Tales of the Riverbank

A collection of short stories inspired by Westminster—the seat of British government and power for hundreds of years.

From the lobbyist for an international high technology corporation to the disillusioned ex-Minister, and from the wannabe Gonzo journalist to the tired and emotional old MP, everyone has their tales to tell, even though they might be better left untold.

Also by Jerry Fishenden

Non-fiction

After Shock. 2020. (Edited by John Schroeter)

Digitizing Government: understanding and implementing new digital business models. 2014. (With Alan Brown and Mark Thompson)

Mobile apps

London Explorer

London Streets

Tales of the Riverbank

Jerry Fishenden

Illustrated by Clive Edwards

To the many individuals and teams in and around Westminster and Whitehall striving to make the UK a better place—often against near impossible odds. And in memory of those friends and colleagues lost along the way.

ꝭ The Tales ꝭ

Tales of the Riverbank

The Old MP

Emmanuel Horatio Fedderby MP was pissed. Not just slightly tipsy, but that stage of room-waltzing kaleidoscopic inebriation where attempting to fly or skip across the Thames, or call a national radio show with confessions of running naked through Poundland while snorting Class A drugs, feel like the best ideas a man can ever have.

And now, not only was he irredeemably intoxicated after his long, gratifyingly indulgent day of excess consumption in the bars and eateries of the Palace of Westminster, but he also needed an actual piss. Right here, and right now.

To Fedderby's horror however, he had somehow exited Stranger's bar onto the crowded riverside terrace instead of his anticipated destination— the merciful sanctuary of the Gents. He looked around in panic, fearful that his distended bladder was about to burst and send a warm and incriminating stain oozing inquisitively through his trousers.

Fortunately, he was in luck. Everyone else was equally drunk or preoccupied on the House of Commons terrace. Nobody would notice. He could indulge in his much-needed urgent self-relief if he was quick and discreet.

"Mum's the word," he slurred, burped and hiccupped to himself.

Fedderby unzipped his fly and moved to the edge of the terrace just in time to send a glistening, bejewelled plume of steaming fluid arcing high through the air. He watched, swaying and mesmerised by the dancing, shimmering stream caught like rare exotic gems in the golden hues of the Pugin lamps.

"Ahhhhhh!" he exclaimed. And then louder: "Ahhhhhhhhhh!"

Life was good. No other feeling on earth was quite so self-gratifyingly satisfying as this.

It was only at this moment of near transcendental personal ecstasy that his attention drifted towards the familiar, costumed figure of the Speaker of the Commons, resting wearily against the nearby wall.

For a fleeting second, Fedderby had the briefest of brief hopes that the Speaker had somehow failed to notice him in the orgasmic act of munificent urinary release. A hope that might well have prevailed—if, that is, Fedderby's aim had not unaccountably drifted from its original trajectory. Now, far from replenishing the dark and brooding waters of dear old Father Thames, his bountiful, dancing necklace of ejected bodily fluid found itself unaccountably drenching the Speaker in a provocative violation of Erskine May.

What to do? An amusing quip? A change of aim? Feign indifference and pretend not to notice? If there had been time, perhaps he could have phoned the Clerk's Department for expert procedural advice.

At that moment, Mother Nature mercifully intervened.

Emmanuel Horatio Fedderby MP wilted, insensible and comatose, to the ground, emitting a loud and resonant underwater bubbler of a fart train in the process.

The Speaker observed Fedderby's trumpeting demise with disdain, doing his best to ignore the unwelcome warmth of the fluid penetrating slowly through his costume and into his skin. The time had long since passed, it seemed, when Members knew how to handle their drink.

"Nothing to see here," the Speaker murmured sharply under his breath as he stepped away, feeling unpleasantly moist and leaving a trail of damp, Lucozade-coloured footprints in his wake. "Not now, anyway."

It was, after all, simply another routine night on the Commons terrace.

There was nothing to be done. A brief curling of the lip and the adoption of a dismissive sneer would have to suffice.

He headed back towards the Speaker's private apartment. Was he, he wondered—and not for the first time—the only one around here who was sober?

The Industry Lobbyist (Part 1)

J ulie Jangles-Daley, Chief Government Lobbyist at the high-tech corporation Mañana International, paced impatiently beside the multifunction office device before scooping up and reading through the first few pages of the draft press release.

"Oh shit!" she pronounced. "Shit, shit, shit, shit." And then—after she'd collected and considered her thoughts more carefully—"Shit-itty-shit!"

She perched on the edge of a desk, grabbed a large red marker pen and started to strike out words and entire paragraphs from the text.

"No-no-NOOOOO!" she exclaimed in despair.

What the hell were the public relations team at EGO, the technology trade association, snorting? Their press release was a sycophantic, lettuce-limp acceptance of the government's provocative new policy on open source software.

Once again it was she, Julie Jangles-Daley (Top 10 Award-Winning

Government Influencer™), who would have to dictate what the technology industry thought. She who would stiffen its backbone and establish clearly their single authoritative voice. She who would force the government to rethink their ridiculous endorsement of the communist-inspired idea of open source and free—*free!*—software for the masses. She who would send the government whimpering and scurrying away from the immense power and unfathomable wealth of the technology industry's off-shore, tax-avoiding oligopoly, just as she'd done on so many previous occasions.

Overcome with rage at the unfairness of it all, she screwed up the entire EGO document in disgust and threw it impatiently towards the overflowing recycling bin. She took her Mañana NattyMobile™ 5.31 phone from her bag, and stabbed impatiently at the spider web shattered SupaStrength™ glass of its touch insensitive screen.

Nothing. She prodded again with renewed urgency. Still nothing. And then the phone illuminated into life:

`Security patches available — downloading!`

The screen briefly displayed a grinning animated badger before hanging and ignoring her frantic stabbing fingers.

"Patches? PATCHES! Oh, choose your bloody moment why don't you? It's not like I've got anything important going on in my life right now is it!?" she shouted, taking a second mobile phone from a rival Big Corporation out of her bag and jabbing ever more angrily until it connected her to EGO's head office.

"Francois. It's Julie. Julie Jangles-Daley. Yes, I'm on my other phone. The one that works. This draft press release you sent me, I wish I had the incredible way with words your team has. No, you idiot. EXTREME SARCASM ALERT! It's shit, complete shambling shit with a capital bold S. I'm sending you a new one, one with balls. Balls as big and hairy as a rampaging Yeti on acid. Tell your pathetic press office to shred their neo-Marxist simpering shit. It's we, the industry, who set government technology policy, not over-promoted jobsworths in Whitehall!"

Pause.

"Yes-yes-yes, the Cardamom Club later would be perfect. And do me a favour. Stick our bill on the small business tab for once will you? It's time they made themselves useful, the little upstart parasites."

She slammed the phone down on the desk and reached for her Mañana

TuchScrean Arty™ (International Corporate Edition) Laptop 2.3.4. She momentarily caught sight of the brilliantly inspired press release she'd been drafting before the screen turned a deep and distinctly unwelcome blue:

```
System Error 0x8847834787348134878374e. Ooops! Hey,
we're real sorry about any inconvenience. An ickle
lickle reboot is required ☺
```

"Now this—THIS!—I really do NOT need!"

Jangles-Daley arrived early for her meeting with the Minister to discover the Department for Business Interference and Bureaucracy (BIB) on Victoria Street overflowing with delegates attending the annual International Administrative Form Design trade fair. She stared in disbelief at the agenda displayed on the walls, wondering what possible value attendees found in seminars including 'Zen and the Art of Administration', 'Basic Principles of Feng Shui with Comic Sans' and 'The Unconscious Bias and Imperial Hegemony of Times New Roman'.

The long queue was barely moving. Patience not being one of her more notable qualities, Jangles-Daley pushed to the front where the reception staff became visibly irritated, resentful of her attempts to interrupt their crucial discussion about the previous night's TV. They barked short hostile retorts at her before finally giving in and providing an 'Escorted Visitor—keep an eye on this one' security pass.

Half an hour late for her appointment she was shown up to the Minister's office. Several additional precious minutes were wasted dealing with truculent resistance from his team of irritating officials before she was finally left alone to talk privately with the Minister, free of the spectre of incriminatory formal minutes.

Michael Dimswick, Minister of State for BIB, was a steadfast and loyal ally of Mañana International. He admired the company's selfless charitable ethos and its diligent and well-publicised commitment every Christmas to help the poor and needy. Without fail, and with far less publicity and razzmatazz, their annual festive generosity included an extravagant hamper of fine wines, luxury food and the latest Mañana merchandise thoughtfully hand-delivered to his own country estate.

He felt it essential to the country's economic prosperity that Mañana and other big international corporations were left free to operate easily and effectively in the UK—even if it did sometimes prove politically awkward to explain why their contracting and finance departments were located in Ireland, where they also declared their surprisingly minuscule profits. But what did he know, a mere Business Minister? 'Big business operates in mysterious ways, their wonders to behold,' as he liked to say, without being quite sure what it meant.

Given his portfolio, Dimswick felt it entirely appropriate to welcome Big Business to the top table. It had a natural right to shape—no—to steer—no—to *inform* government policy. But not nearly so much as he believed in the future career potential of cosying up to Big Business.

Big Business always has Big Fat Jobs with Big Fat Salaries and Big Fat Expense Budgets. Many of the most lucrative jobs were to be found at the very top of the executive management tree for those with excellent political connections, where lack of experience—or indeed an absence of any discernible expertise, competence or moral compass—were no impediment to appointment. Lucrative sinecure opportunities wining and dining as an 'adviser to the board'—a well-paid, ill-defined and largely theatrical role—were therefore always a natural, and popular, post-political career choice.

"Michael. It's *so* good to see you," smarmed Jangles-Daley.

"Likewise. My favourite Top 10 lobbyist. And what can I do for you today, Julie?"

She paused a moment for dramatic effect. And then: "We have a problem."

"We do?"

"The Cabinet Office. It's irritating me."

"Oh, the Cabinet Office irritates everyone. Don't take it personally."

They laughed.

"Nothing useful ever comes out of the Cabinet Office, Julie. Everyone knows that."

"Perhaps so, Michael. But they're taking an irrational, anti-business stance. It's hugely damaging."

"Well, what do you expect, Julie? It's overrun with digital geeks prancing around in shorts and T-shirts, posting stickers on the walls, playing Twister, sporting fundamentalist beard-fluff and cycling to work on pimped-up Bromptons. They all spout the same nonsense about a 'digital revolution' as if it's the second coming of the Messiah. It's so tedious."

"Oh, it's far worse than that Michael. They're exhibiting deeply damaging and anti-competitive behaviour. Our new NattyMobile™ 5.31 has been banned simply because it uses exclusive innovations based on our extensively researched and patented proprietary technology. They have this obsession about everything being 'open' you see."

"Open?"

"Yes, it sounds preposterous I know. Open standards, open source, open markets, open competition. A whole heap of 'open' nonsense."

"Oh, how absurd! Big business certainly didn't get where it is today by being open, Julie. And neither of course did government."

"Exactly."

"That's today's civil service for you I'm afraid. They don't provide much of a service and I don't find many of them terribly civil either to be frank. You've no idea how hard it is to be a Minister in Whitehall and get anything done, Julie. They seem to think they're here to stop us. They impede our manifesto programme far more effectively than the official opposition."

"We invest a lot of time and resources in the UK, Michael. We employ a lot of people, including in some very marginal political constituencies. *Very marginal constituencies.*"

"Ah. Point taken. Duly noted. We're very grateful, Julie, you know that."

"Mañana is a generous and patient company. But there are limits to our patience, Michael. We may reconsider any future UK investments if your government continues to make business difficult for us."

"Difficult? Oh, we'd certainly never want that, Julie."

"Then make that clear to the Cabinet Office. Remove their proposed hippy blockade of our new NattyMobile™ 5.31. They need to be taught who's in charge around here, Michael, and it certainly isn't them. They can't be allowed to buck the market. We're a revered member of the International Masonic Oligopoly of Big Technology Companies for good reason and we have every intention of keeping it that way."

"Of course, Julie. Of course. I shall have a discreet word with the Prime Minister. He's a good friend. A *very* good friend. We'll put a stop to this nonsense. I guarantee it. Trust me."

Scuttle

Edwin Scuttle, Director General of Internal Security (Designate) at
the Hostile Office, looked at his morning newspaper with disbelief.
No, he wasn't misreading it—it was right there in front of him in
bold black and white:

HOSTILE SECRETARY RELAXES CONTROL ORDERS

Incredible. He stared in disbelief. Again. There was, after all, never too
much disbelief one can have when busy waging the War Against Terror—or
WAT as it is better known to perfidious security industry insiders and allied
masonic lodges. How many times had he explained to the Hostile Secretary—
very slooooow-ly and very pe-dant-ic-ally, so that even she could
understand—'Never do anything—anything!—without my express
permission first, okay love?'

He slammed the desk with clenched fists and howled in dismay. When would these feeble, voter-obsessed politicians learn to fall into line and do as they were instructed? How hard could it be? Why were they so obsessed with being popular and playing to the crowd rather than Doing the Right Thing?

It had taken Scuttle years to build up the fear of the Fear of Terrorism in the British public. Years to whip up the media into a frothing, foaming frenzy of hyperbolic articles cringing with trepidation about foreign looking chaps with wispy beards and bald heads. Did anyone have any idea how difficult it was to cultivate and sustain a conspiracy of lies and paranoia at the centre of government?

It was time to regain momentum, to re-establish an eviscerating sense of fear and foreboding. He needed to force the Hostile Secretary back into the exact same state of docility and subservient toadying compliance with his agenda as every other useful quockerwodger before her.

There had only ever been one maverick exception, one utter deviant of a Hostile Secretary who'd failed to accommodate his perfectly reasonable demands. A loathsome, independent-minded miscreant who'd even dared to proclaim that Scuttle's office was 'not fit for purpose' and that his motives were deeply subversive and from the 'dark side'.

Scuttle had organised his downfall quickly and efficiently. A series of carefully staged 'difficulties' at border control and an artfully contrived backlog of passport applications soon saw angry citizens queueing for hours and calling for the Minister's head. The resulting big font headlines in the lapdog tabloid press were sufficient to erode and destroy the Minister's reputation, resulting in his rapid expulsion from office.

The best Hostile Secretaries knew their place and did as they were told, beholden to Scuttle's spell and command. Domesticated and house-trained politicians, the ones who endlessly spouted his scripted guff about the 'War on Terrorism' and 'strong borders' and a 'hostile environment', he would generously allow to enjoy a long tenure, as any fule in Whitehall kno.

Scuttle considered himself the strict but fair disciplinarian father of a troubled and dysfunctional family. The fickle public were his wayward feral children—children in urgent need of robust guidance and correction. He was not about to let a transient goody-two-shoes, here today and gone tomorrow politician, deflect him from his lifetime's mission.

"Under the close and careful supervision of my thumb," he whispered to himself, and smiled, snatching up the phone to talk to one of Whitehall's trusted inner circle of good people.

"Morlock? It's Scuttle. Invoke Plan C. Release Akbar. We need a state of heightened anxiety. Let's ramp up the fear and keep it ramped up. Make sure the usual dimwit hacks get their spurious security briefing so they feel loved and special. Remind me, what's the name of that useful idiot, the one who writes those ridiculous 'real life' spy books and claims to know about intelligence and cybercrime? Ah, that's him. Give the security chundering dunce the usual nonsense. The media love him, assume he knows what he's talking about. We need the standard wall-to-wall, front-page, arse-licking, sensationalist coverage."

He terminated the call and sat back in his Senior Civil Service (SCS) Swivel Chair™ (second edition, patents pending). Plan C was simple and quite, quite beautiful. Later today Akbar would be released. He was an innocent suspect previously arrested in a badly botched, but high-profile, counter-terrorism operation. His arrest had been dramatically and breathlessly splashed across the TV evening news, providing a carefully timed story about how Akbar had *access to terrorist materials'* and was discovered with *'sophisticated computer equipment'* in his possession.

The media were rarely diligent about enquiring precisely what such apparently incriminating phrases meant. Had they done so, they might have been surprised to learn the rather less dramatic reality: Akbar was a home broadband subscriber with internet access which he *could* have used to research extremist information (*'access to terrorist materials'*—better described as being able to use Google search). And he also owned an ageing iPad (the *'sophisticated computer equipment'*).

Akbar's detention and the woeful acquiescence of the media in bigging it up achieved the precise outcome Scuttle desired. Sensationalist terrorist-related headlines dominated the news at the ideal moment during the passage through Parliament of yet another Bill to curtail citizens' freedoms. MPs and Peers alike were bluffed, frightened and stampeded into hurriedly passing the legislation without adequate evidence, scrutiny and debate.

Now it was the turn of Plan C. Today's special announcement—Akbar's release from custody and his disclosure as a supergrass. It was a feel-good news story, providing a small but important propaganda victory in the ongoing WAT. Terror by press release was proving one of Scuttle's more effective innovations.

The reality however shared nothing in common with the perception Scuttle was artfully creating. As an entirely innocent victim of a mistaken hostile arrest, Akbar knew absolutely nothing about terrorism, or indeed any terrorists. He wasn't even particularly good at using Google and remained far from certain about how to install apps on his iPad without his young daughter's help. But none of these trivial factual details mattered. Akbar's release would be accompanied by histrionic revelations about how he'd furnished the security forces with compelling insider information, exposing an extensive terrorist network and imminent national threat.

This PR triumph would help Scuttle persuade the Hostile Secretary she'd been badly mistaken to show any personal initiative, and dangerously foolish in diluting and disregarding his earlier recommendations. She, the Prime Minister and the media would all soon be knee-jerking like demented marionettes once again, baying with their predictable rabid demands for tougher laws and mindlessly parroting 'Something must be done!' and 'Nothing to hide, nothing to fear!'

Scuttle would re-establish himself as the puppet master supreme, the benevolent guiding hand behind the construction of the protective state. A state with a deep, ubiquitous insight into every living moment of every person in the UK, providing the benevolent direction, care, intervention and correction they required, whether they wanted it or not. He would not so much move the Overton window as rip it from its frame.

As part of his plan, Scuttle had enthusiastically sponsored the development of the Hostile Office Holistic Operations (HOHO) system. And what a system it had become, providing an unprecedented surveillance breakthrough inside the department. HOHO busily mined and collated a vast diaspora of sensitive and valuable information previously well-secured in an array of separate systems—from borders to policing to immigration—applying all the latest new-fangled technologies of machine learning and artificial intelligence.

It was unfortunate perhaps that in the process of its implementation HOHO had mistakenly exposed the identities of various undercover law and enforcement officials, police informants, intelligence agency employees, and witness protection programme individuals and their new lives. But such ephemeral inconveniences were only to be expected in the process of digitisation and modernisation: 'Success depends upon sacrifice—particularly the sacrifice of others,' as Scuttle liked to say.

Now HOHO was being scaled up to suck data out of all Whitehall's systems, eliminating previously separate and secure data silos and identifying every social deviant, and anticipated deviant, who needed to be proactively outed and dealt with. This was the true pinnacle of the digital age. It was a godsend for Scuttle, accelerating his plans in ways he'd once thought impossible and enabling him to implement powerful, constitution-changing reforms.

'Revolution not evolution indeed,' he muttered to himself with delight.

At this very moment the pan-government digital team was busy building on the success of HOHO to implement a set of centralised computer platforms, providing a single point of insight into everyone's interactions with government, central and local. Every tax they paid, every benefit they claimed, every website page they looked at, every report they downloaded, every message they received. Supplementing this pioneering hosepipe of information was a set of external feeds drawn from telecoms companies, social media, blog posts, articles, conference speeches and research papers.

The results flowed directly into the Master Analytics Dashboard, visualising in near real-time every government initiative and programme the Parliamentary opposition parties and civil society organisations were accessing and researching. It enabled Scuttle and the inner Whitehall network of good people to stay one step ahead. To anticipate and neutralise their counter-attacks and criticisms of government policy long before they had any chance of success. It was Scuttle's perfect, big, wet digital dream come true.

But his biggest joy of all was his ingenious 'Foreigners Unsettled Status' smartphone app. At the flick of a digital switch he could instantly remove the legitimacy of someone's legal status, evicting them from the UK or preventing them re-entering if they were foolish enough ever to leave its borders. Software was eating democracy, giving him powers that didn't exist in the pre-internet age. It was all so much easier than the traditional and long-established Hostile Office practices of 'mislaying', falsifying or accidentally bulk-shredding paperwork.

'Oh brave new world that has such technology in it,' he mused.

Scuttle's epiphany occurred over a decade earlier, the sobering revelation that it had fallen to him, and him alone, to rescue the increasingly wayward UK and redirect it onto a better path. Just as schoolchildren were registered, monitored, tracked and kept under surveillance every minute of their learning day, those same well-proven benefits would now be extended beyond the playground boundaries to the so-called adult population.

Scuttle's task was well advanced. He was busy entrenching the technical architecture and subservient culture essential to this brave new world, artfully constructing his all-seeing digital panopticon one Parliamentary Bill after another. The result was a quiet, backroom shift of power on a scale unseen since the Civil War, removing the constitutional protections and levers from the increasingly superfluous Whitehall departments and slowly, one jigsaw bit and byte at a time, transferring them to the central digital platforms—and hence to him. And all without any meaningful democratic scrutiny or debate.

"Softly, softly, catchee monkey."

Scuttle had learned long ago that ascending to the right position within a bureaucracy, manipulating and directing it from the inside, was far more certain of success than overt external political acts. Shouty, high-profile activism and civil society pressure were all very well, but in reality they were futile, empty gestures, mere acts of theatre. Real change, and the terror required to catalyse and enforce it, can only come from within the system itself, aided and abetted by the glories of the digital revolution.

"For the WAT," he murmured.

Time for a well-deserved sherry.

The Rocking Entrepreneur

Bob Rover, Chief Geek-at-Large at Mañana International, listened with growing impatience and frustration to the product team. It was well over two years since he'd promised the world a major breakthrough, a revolution in speech synthesis and voice recognition technology.

In a few days' time, he'd be jetting to the UK for a series of high-profile meetings, supporting Chief Operating Officer Gary Bunter in a busy outreach schedule, including appointments with the British Prime Minister. Rover wanted to deliver on his earlier announcement by breaking exclusive news during his visit that Mañana International was about to revolutionise technology and leapfrog its competitors yet again.

Rover was recognised globally as one of the smartest of high-tech billionaires. His meteoric rise to fame and fortune came startlingly early in his career after he secured international patents for any computing device that hung, crashed or rebooted itself at the most irritating and inconvenient moment for users. This brilliant innovation ensured that any time any technology anywhere in the world showed a blank screen, failed or randomly rebooted it was *Kerching!* time for Rover and Mañana International. More money flowed into Mañana's coffers than any other company in history.

Without Rover's technical eureka moment and pedantic knowledge of international patent law, Mañana would have been just another dull technology wannabe in the marketplace. Instead, he'd driven his company from small start-up to the biggest and best high-tech business on the planet. Many enraged swivel-eyed competitors had gone bust in their vainglorious attempts to rival Mañana, their leaders too busy ranting and railing at Rover and his unstoppable success to remember to keep a steady hand safely on the tiller of their own ill-fated businesses.

Now, as he listened to the meandering presentation from the product group, Rover began to rock gently forwards and backwards in his chair. Far from hearing welcome news of a breakthrough success, he found himself listening instead to a series of miserable and long-winded excuses about why the revolution he'd promised would not be happening. Again.

"The voice recognition algorithms are not performing as well with real users as they did in the usability lab."

"Oh. So tell me now, why is that?" enquired Rover quietly, his intense gaze an indication of a slowly burning inner fuse to those who knew him well.

"Er, we think," the lead product manager prevaricated. "We think it's to do with accents. Different accents."

"You think? I need data. Facts. Evidence. We don't make technical or investment decisions based on casual opinions or idle speculation."

"Well, to be more precise, there are complications arising from different geographies, behaviours and ethnographies."

Rover raised his eyebrows, his gentle rocking backwards and forwards becoming slightly more pronounced.

"Our initial lab tests were not sufficiently representative of the diversity encountered in a live, contemporary and contextual multicultural domain."

"English, plain English please. You mean to tell me your voice recognition program doesn't work in the real world?"

"Er, no."

"You had one job. One job. It wasn't a difficult request. To develop technology that recognises and responds to spoken commands. One that lets users talk to their desktop and mobile computers instead of using keyboards and mice and touch screens."

"Yes, I know but—"

"Our competitors are humiliating us. We're falling years behind. Tell me, who precisely did you use in your earlier tests?"

"Er, well we engaged an extensive portfolio of colleagues from right across our division."

Rover sighed. His rocking stepped up another notch. "You tested your code with a monolithic bunch of male white computer engineers. Yet only now do you appreciate the world is more diverse? That not everyone speaks with the same accent, talks the same way, comes from the same background? That not everyone in the world is as monocultural and as stupid as your team?"

"Um, well, I guess that's sort of about the size of it, Mr Rover. But—"

"Get out of here."

"I'm sss-sorry?"

"Get out," Rover repeated quietly.

"Get out?" enquired the product manager hesitantly, wondering if he'd possibly misheard.

Rover reached peak manoeuvre, rocking significantly backwards and forwards in his chair. This was not a good sign. His management team gently eased themselves further away to give Rover more room, vacating the immediate danger zone.

"You heard me. I hate—HATE—having to repeat myself. You seem to have major problems understanding the most elementary of instructions."

The product manager flushed crimson and moved towards the door, followed closely by his senior staff, dragging their half-shut laptops, a dodgy flip-chart tripod and a scattering of sticky notes with them.

"Could we have one more—"

"Get. The. Fuck. Out. Of. Here."

And as Rover commanded, so was it done. The room remained silent for a time, apart from Rover's heavy breathing as he rocked intensely, backwards and forwards, backwards and forwards, in his chair. Rocking. Rocking. Rocking.

"Where do we find these people? Where do we find them?"

The room remained silent. His staff hoped it was a rhetorical question. Either way, it was going unanswered.

The Chief Scientific Adviser

P rofessor Polly Quibble was one of the leading climatologists of her generation. Her insight, knowledge and professional expertise would have been perfectly exploited working as an adviser on international climate change—somewhere such as the Department for Perpetual Environmental and Rural Announcements for example.

This was precisely why she'd been appointed instead to the Hostile Office as its Chief Scientific Adviser. Here she found herself considering matters of a complex technical nature ranging from biometrics to encryption—subjects about which she had zero knowledge or experience. She was, quite simply, entirely out of her professional comfort zone.

This was, of course, exactly as it was intended to be. The misplacement of scientific advisers around Whitehall is a long established, highly optimised and much venerated tradition. It facilitates the smooth running of government by ensuring anyone with expertise is kept well away from departments handling policy related to their subject area. The last thing politicians need is a knowledgeable professional breathing down their necks and humiliating them by pointing out errors, omissions and 'economies with the actualité' in their crowd-pleasing, vote-manipulating emanations.

Quibble was busy preparing for her imminent appearance before the House of Commons committee stage review of the draft Interception of Private Life (Citizens) Bill. In front of her was a printout of the Bill, annotated and interleaved with a stack of colourful sticky notes, and alongside it the voluminous and verbose guidance provided by senior Hostile Office officials.

Over recent months, Quibble had attended endless lengthy Whitehall meetings to discuss the Bill. Meetings where officials repeatedly reassured her of their domain expertise and insight. Meetings so successful in fact that often there'd not even been enough chairs for everyone to sit on. Yes, *that* successful.

The guidance was a godsend, although she was slightly puzzled why substantial chunks appeared to be verbatim excerpts from Wikipedia. The briefing notes spelt out jargon such as 'computer', 'app', 'data', 'smartphone', 'software' and so on—a compendium of obscure and deeply pompous mumbo-jumbo. Let's face it, technology wasn't proper science, was it? Computers were nothing more than a fancy-pants abacus, and technology just an upstart teenage delinquent sulking moodily on the edge of science, left outside the grown-ups' laboratory to play with bunting and balloons.

'Data is everything that isn't data,' she read from the Bill. Was that right? It sounded like nonsense. She re-read it for more information, but without becoming any the wiser. She sighed. There were times when she wondered why she bothered. Was this really why she'd spent so many years devoting her every waking moment to studying and researching how best to save humanity from its selfish and suicidal destruction of the planet?

A few hours later Quibble was in the Upper Committee Corridor of the Houses of Parliament, standing awkwardly before the committee Clerk.

"Keep your answers brief and to the point," the Clerk advised. "We'll be in open session with the public and media present, and live on Parliament TV."

Quibble was relieved she'd prepared so thoroughly and drew solace from the knowledge she wouldn't be facing the committee alone. Alongside her would be Babcock Legrande Dick, Programme Director of the Nudge-Nudge Directorate (Citizens' Unit) at the Hostile Office. They nodded briefly at each other, entered the room and took their seats, facing the intimidating horseshoe of irritable looking committee members.

The session started. Quibble and Legrande Dick briefly introduced themselves, setting out their respective roles and responsibilities. The Chair looked up from her papers and gave a fleeting smile.

"Good afternoon and welcome," she said, deceptively disarmingly. "Thank you for attending today's session on the Interception of Private Life (Citizens) Bill. We want to explore and understand your expert knowledge on the technical aspects and feasibility of the Bill, and look forward to hearing your professional insight, Professor Quibble."

Quibble shifted awkwardly in her chair and shuffled an assortment of sticky notes in what she hoped was an authoritative and convincing manner.

"In particular," continued the Chair. "We're concerned about the deep technical implications of the Bill and the idea of an independent oversight panel. Perhaps we could start with your views on that?"

Quibble cleared her throat.

"Of course, Chair. A technical oversight panel, or an authoritative advisory board if you prefer, is something many organisations have. It could be consulted often—or not of course, depending upon needs and requirements. Whether a consultation happens with such a panel, which should be diverse in its composition and not permitted any mission creep in terms of scope, is not in itself any indication of whether it is a good panel, or a bad panel, so to speak, but merely a sign that there may, or may not, be issues for it to be consulted upon."

The Chair and Members stared at her blankly. Quibble interpreted this as a sign of encouragement. They were doubtless impressed and unnerved by her newly acquired domain knowledge and sticky note insights, combined with her signature and authoritative plain-speaking. And yet a little voice was nagging at her deep inside, making her hesitate. She'd previously observed a disconcerting tendency for committee witnesses to become obscurely prolix and discursive rather than directly answering questions. Naturally, she wasn't foolish enough to fall into that particular trap herself—or was she? This uncharacteristic and troublesome doubt was making her surprisingly self-conscious.

"If I might add a remark, Chair," her fellow witness Legrande Dick interjected. "It would be highly inappropriate were such a panel to impede the necessary and essential workings of the Hostile Office. My expert colleague Professor Quibble, describes the matter precisely, succinctly and well."

"You think so?" The Chair swatted him away. "But we are more interested in the technical aspects. We shall come to our wider concerns regarding the perpetual failings of the incompetent Hostile Office in due course. In the absence of an expert technical panel, have you, as the Chief Scientific Adviser, been the primary source of contact and review, Professor Quibble?"

"Yes. I work very closely with my departmental colleagues, and have attended a multitude of meetings where this Bill has been discussed, re-written and refined. A great deal of work has gone into its creation. My presence ensures that colleagues can access the necessary scientific and technical knowledge. Although perhaps I should at this point make a small confession."

"Which is?" prompted the Chair.

"I think that Babcock—Mr Legrande Dick—and his colleagues understand far more about all of this than anyone else. I'm very impressed with the sophisticated technical jargon they use with such ease and familiarity, despite it being complex and often indeed multisyllabic—polysyllabic even— in nature. They have diligently consulted with numerous very big technology companies who comprehend this sort of thing, and also with big suppliers and their very important experts with senior executive, even vice-presidential, titles, who've given freely and generously of their time.

"These meetings have been both impressive and informative, including an extended, open discussion about how to nudge-nudge citizens' personal lives without them being aware we've done so. While I cannot confess to have understood everything discussed, at its core it must be relatively simple—it is mere technology not science we're talking about here after all, full of obscure and quite frankly meaningless acronyms to provide it with a false sense of importance. Despite this, everything I've heard has sounded convincing to me and overall a 'Good Thing'."

One of the committee members leaned forward.

"Professor Quibble. The internet, indeed, much of the digital commerce we take for granted in our private lives, depends on electronic protection.

This is achieved, as I'm sure you're aware, through encryption. Yet I see a reference to its removal. How can it possibly be right that compromising encryption, the online security essential to aspects of our daily lives such as personal banking, is being proposed?"

"Oh." Quibble laughed. "I must counsel caution. Encryption is, for those of you who do not know—and I expect there are many of you in that category here today—a sort of scramble-egging and hash-tagging of things, if I can express it in layman's terms. Without it, as you say, it would become difficult to use technology securely and safely. But the Bill is not removing encryption. No, not at all. It's removing electronic protection. These are very different things. Very different indeed."

"How precisely do they differ?" the committee member persisted.

Quibble was starting to feel uneasy. She looked down and shuffled the sticky notes around the table, as if trying to complete a complex jigsaw puzzle. It was only now becoming clearer to her why committee witnesses often chose to provide opaque, rambling and inconclusive responses—anything in preference to volunteering information that might not stand up to scrutiny and hence provoke another barrage of awkward and penetrating questions.

"Well, it's not removing encryption, but removing electronic protection."

"Professor Quibble. You can say that phrase as many times as you like, but frankly I've no idea what you mean."

"Well that doesn't come as any great surprise," Quibble responded shortly. "These are complex technical matters. I've spent many, many months listening to them being discussed. I hardly think we can expect you to understand them in a matter of minutes at a superficial meeting of jack-of-all-trades random members of Parliament such as this."

There was an icy glare from the Committee chair which Quibble failed to notice.

"All the ridiculous nonsense talked by self-serving, so-called experts about 'back doors' and breaking encryption and blahdy-blahdy-blah!" she continued. "No-one wants that insecure type of thing. No-one. We're proposing the capability to access what we need to access, once we've obtained a so-called warrant through the bureaucratic inconvenience of due legal process of course.

"So, you see, there is no threat to the integrity of encryption here, but only electronic protection. Companies and people using the internet utilise numerous different technologies—covering what we call 'hardware' and 'software', if you'll excuse my use of deeply technical jargon which doubtless sounds like so much double-Dutch to lay people such as yourselves—and there are many different layers of protection that could be removed when the need arises."

"But not encryption?" the committee member enquired.

"Electronic protection." Quibble had settled on this comforting phrase and felt it worth repeating. As often as necessary. "We cannot miscast this as 'removing encryption' when there are many different options within the scope of the Bill."

"You seem flustered Professor Quibble," the Chair commented.

"Nonsense! It's exceptionally difficult to determine the best and most elementary language to use to explain myself to rank amateurs and novices."

There was a lengthy silence.

"You believe snooping will be possible if this 'electronic protection' as you call it can be implemented, but without breaking encryption?"

"I object strongly to the term 'snooping'," Legrande Dick intervened irritably. "One may tolerate a certain amount of ignorant fear-mongering from doom-laden naysayers in the privileged and remote corridors of academia and so-called civil society, but I don't expect juvenile and frankly crass behaviour from this committee. 'Snooping' is not a term we recognise in the Hostile Office. It's not in our organisational lexicon or cultural value system."

"And never will it be," added Quibble. "We're not snooping, but merely applying powers set out in the Bill. Snooping is not a good thing, people wouldn't like it. It implies that government officials are intruding into the general public's private affairs invasively, furtively, pruriently and inappropriately. That is most certainly not what we are planning. Not at all."

"No?" asked the Chair, raising her eyebrows.

"No. The Bill allows us to know when people are looking at things that they should *not* be looking at. This is an essential distinction. Snooping, by contrast, is underhand and to be frowned at with distaste. The Bill has very strict safeguards to prevent it. I'm sorry to go well beyond my own specialist scientific remit, and in such technical detail, but this distinction is important."

"Apparently so," sighed the Committee Chair. "Apparently so."

The Old Parliamentary Press Bar

The old Parliamentary press bar had been a treasured and much-loved symbol of a bygone time. A vibrant reminder of an age when Fleet Street gloried in its influence and status as the Fourth Estate. The bar's prestigious position at the heart of the House of Commons, situated within convenient and timely staggering distance of the Press Gallery of the debating chamber, was a proud and important signifier of its status.

The old bar was an intimate and relatively extravagant affair, carved from light oak in the finest mock Augustus Pugin. At its best, it was a lively, rumbustious and collegiate place where journalists, MPs, Peers and Officers and staff of both the House of Commons and House of Lords rubbed shoulders, burnished gossip and became gloriously and repeatedly legless on cheap drinks long into many an evening.

Around its walls, totemic wooden panels dutifully recorded the names of the chosen few, the annually elected Chairmen of the Press Gallery, their names embellished in proud gilt lettering like the noble fallen heroes of a forgotten war. The press bar was a unique, alcoholic crucible at the heart of the Royal Palace where many a political career was made or broken, where idle gossip or the leak of confidential documents and insider secrets became the next day's front-page headlines, and where many a relationship was forged—or fucked, foundered and forgotten.

But Winter had come to the old press bar, part of a more widespread and profound climate change that sent a frosty, hostile wind through Parliament and the press, sweeping away its oldest and most valued traditions and places. Successive governments had grown progressively angrier and displeased with the media, eager to outsource blame and responsibility for their countless self-inflicted woes onto the messenger instead. It was a far easier political deflection than owning up to their own vacuity, half-truths, cockups and serial equivocation and incompetence.

Neither did the conspicuously garrulous Speaker of the House—an exaggeratedly colourful and loquacious character seemingly displaced from the pages of a Charles Dickens discarded first draft—appreciate the way the media criticised him. They portrayed him as a vain narcissist, and denigrated his attempts to modernise Parliament by suggesting it was more accurately an exercise in gifting himself ever more power, privilege and status.

This unholy alliance of a disgruntled government and a Parliamentary Speaker ripe with braggadocio had not been a good thing. As a result, vengeance had been taken. Change had been imposed.

The Press Must Know Its Place.

This season of intolerance saw the old press bar permanently shuttered, an act of vengeance camouflaged behind the smokescreen of 'progress'. Its wannabe Pugin woodwork was hurriedly dismantled and placed into storage, as if in amateur tribute to the final scene of 'Raiders of the Lost Ark', where the Ark is crated and shelved inside a large, anonymous government facility never to be seen again. The space the bar once occupied became a soulless hot-desking area, the ultimate, and intentional, insult to the spirit—in every sense—of what stood there before.

And then, phoenix-like, a new press bar, nicknamed 'Good-griefs', was fashioned nearby. A bar so calculatedly anodyne and antiseptic that it made a rude and unmistakable public statement about the authorities' fear and loathing of the media, and just how low its once ascendant star had fallen. Created in a loveless, cheerless corridor, it deliberately echoed the stained, Formica-topped service counter of a British Rail era train, a characterless, hostile space cursed with bright fluorescent lighting and devoid of any vestige of status or warmth.

The former humanity and intimacy and prestige and entire purpose of the press bar were lost. The historic wooden Press Gallery panels listing its illustrious Chairmen were now sneeringly diminished, humiliated by their placement on whitewashed corridor walls and appearing every bit as dignified as gaudy fairground adverts fly-posted on derelict shop windows.

This public and ritual demotion of the press bar, and by extension the press itself, acted as an unwelcome mirror of the declining influence of Fleet Street in an age of online, 24/7 rolling 'news'. Like the old bar, the old press were increasingly being replaced or pensioned off, swept away by the advent of fake news, gossip dressed up as reportage, celebrity bloggers and self-promoting antisocial-media attention seekers with little interest in verification, facts or objectivity. The appetite for the hard, time-consuming work of unearthing evidence and speaking truth to power was fast falling out of fashion, yielding to those interested only in the pursuit of followers guaranteed to obsequiously like and retweet their tribal, fleeting soundbites.

But perhaps the presence of the old Parliamentary press bar is not entirely lost. Staff working late into the evening at the hot-desks where the bar once stood occasionally claim to hear the distant chink of drinking glasses—and the sound of voices raised in laughter and hearty cheer.

The Street Philosopher

Euan Hogan smells. It is the primordial, authentic odour of raw humanity unfiltered and undisguised. A stench that oozes and pervades the air well beyond the immediate space around him, its fetid tendrils reaching out to engage and enrage the nostrils of by-passers many yards distant.

It is the smell that everyone once shamelessly emitted and inhaled in a time and age long since lost. A smell from that now forgotten past before humanity connived to socially distance itself from the remainder of its animal kith and kin with camouflaging scents and perfumes and other means of olfactory misdirection and subterfuge.

Hogan is blissfully unaware and unashamed of his perfectly natural bodily odours. As unaware and unashamed as anyone in the middle ages would have been as they stepped through the shit and piss and animal faeces and decomposing body parts and decaying vegetables and other festering monstrosities that once decorated the streets of great stinking global cities such as London.

He is well acclimatised to his parallel world, his stained, ragged and slowly decomposing clothes near welded to his dusty skin so long has he worn them. His shoes are the fraying, shredding remnants of plastic carrier bags—bags on which he has avoided the environmental surcharge courtesy of the crowding shoppers who discard them thoughtlessly into his own rich repositories, the overflowing rubbish bins of Soho and its many alleys and by-ways.

Most of those who pass him grimace briefly and over-theatrically at the stench, only to then hurry more determinedly on their way with a quickening pace, self-absorbed in the empty busyness of their own lives. And too repelled, or perhaps too frightened, to contemplate how Hogan has ended up in his current state while they, fortuitously, have not. At least, not yet.

Sometimes those passing him do miss a beat and shudder, as if momentarily conscious that the slimmest of wafer-thin chance events separates the falsely comforting veneer of their illusory, sweet-smelling existence from that of Hogan's. In such rare moments of insight, those passing by understand, if only fleetingly, that their own world is not so distant from his as they might like.

Occasionally a kindly soul stops to enquire after Hogan. It is usually a moment of revelation, but more so for them than for him. For while Hogan may reek like a decomposing skunk that's been stuck in a U-bend for months and have all the visual allure of a seagull-curated municipal dump, his mind and personality remain both richer and more alive than those who scamper hurriedly past and scowl irritably in his direction.

Today, Hogan is shuffling at leisure around St. James's Park, enjoying the sunlight and the warmth and the canon of birdsong from the trees and ponds and paths around him. There is the murmur and colour of foreign accents and languages from passing tourists, the joyous squeal of a young child, the linked hands of sauntering lovers, and—inevitably—somewhere an unseen barking dog.

And there are also those oddest of odd creatures, the uniformed businesspeople with their braying voices hurriedly walking in agitated groups between meetings, stridently discussing inconsequential affairs in the nomenclature of nonsense, talking at each other in the hollow grammelot of our age:

"Blah. Blah-dy. Blah. Strategy. Sustainability. Networked effort. Pivot our golden footprint. Differentiating and value-added. Customer centric. Reimagining our optics. Super laser focused. Onwards. Digital first. Synergies. Information radiator. Competitive advantage. User driven. Win-win. Out of the box agility. Big data. Fourth egotistical revolution. Blockchain cognition. Collaborative and innovative. Ecosystem. Capture the upside. Blah. Blah-dy. Blah."

The less they have to contribute to the world, the more they seem to talk, the louder and more boorish and self-promoting their demeanour, and the more meaningless and valueless their language. Their whole lives have become preoccupied with peddling vacuous concepts and jargon parroted from the same script, the identikit stale slides hyped to every gullible victim by the hollow racketeers of the large consultancy and 'research' companies.

Hogan's attention is drawn towards a smart, Westminster type—slightly overweight, expensive suit, coiffured mullet, handmade shoes—lurking by one of the park bins. He hesitates a moment to observe him like an ornithologist encountering a rare bird. While Hogan is wearily accustomed to searching and sorting through the unpredictable detritus of waste deposited daily in London's bins, it's unusual to see one of the exotic Oxbridge-bred species in their full plumage rummaging in such a receptacle.

For a moment Hogan experiences a flash of irrational resentment, even of anger, fearing the portly gent is intent on stealing from the bin the very objects so essential to his own everyday existence. And then Hogan realises his mistake: the well-dressed gent isn't removing items from the bin, but reading hurriedly through papers and then contributing to it. Hogan watches as document after document is considered, frowned over, considered again and then unceremoniously crumpled and dumped.

After a time, the Westminster Suit is done. His pile of papers exhausted, he looks around furtively, stabs clumsily at his phone with surprisingly pale podgy little fingers to make a brief empty call—"Yah, yah, yah"—and then waddles away in the direction of Whitehall.

Hogan waits a moment before moving over to explore the unwanted papers so publicly and indifferently abandoned. He pulls the first crumpled sheet from the top of the bin and straightens it out.

It has an official crest, and is headed 'Intelligence and Security Committee'. And also 'Top Secret'. Surprised, Hogan glances through the document. It contains graphic details of the work of the security agencies and their role in something called 'extraordinary rendition'. Neither 'extraordinary' nor 'rendition' sound like they refer to anything particularly wholesome.

He looks around with unease, wondering if he is making a terrible mistake. Is this a set-up, a sting? Is the Westminster Suit about to waddle hurriedly back into view pointing his expensively manicured sausage-like finger in accusation and calling on undercover police officers to seize him and his glittering magpie treasures?

But no. All remains uneventful in the park. Somewhere the dog still barks. Hogan returns his attention to the bin. There is more. Much more.

A treasury-tagged document referencing terrorist organisations and undercover operations. A note from an intelligence officer defending the use of controversial investigations. A brief from an official in the Hostile Office about a new digital surveillance system. Letters from constituents with detailed family circumstances and problems. A desperate lover's romantic, and surprisingly explicit, illustrated hand-written note containing suggestions for a variety of physically challenging, if not near impossible, positions. The offer of an all-expenses-paid visit to a corrupt Middle Eastern fiefdom for a spurious 'study tour', with all inclusive 'private tuition and one-to-one deeply therapeutic massage'. There is revelation after revelation in this unexpected and astonishing trove.

"Christmas, bloody Christmas," Hogan whispers to himself, recognising this unsolicited miracle for what it is: a much-needed wellspring to maintain him in the exceptionally modest lifestyle to which he's long become accustomed.

He takes from his pocket a vintage Nokia phone, rarely used but invaluable, switches it on and calls an old contact, a trusted Fleet Street journalist from the near-forgotten days when he inhabited the insane and illusory world around him. It is one of those unusual, reluctant moments when he will once again dance clumsily and briefly with the devil, erecting a temporary bridge between his own world and the broken one he left behind.

"Herring? It's Euan. I have something quite extraordinary for you. I think you're going to like it."

The Ambassador

I am sending this note with hopes of great discretion, although based on my experience of the recent series of leaks of previous diplomatic cables to the tabloid press, I trust Number 10's discretion on such matters about as much as a ███████ frog in a ██████████████.

It is with considerable apprehension that I must draw attention to the reprehensible conduct of a senior Whitehall official, a Mr Edwin Scuttle. I have it on good authority that he recently engaged in a series of undisclosed meetings with █████ from ██████████ and █████ from ████████. This is entirely unacceptable, a breach of international etiquette—and, incidentally, UN sanctions. I therefore recommend in the strongest possible terms that a close eye be kept on both him and his questionable agenda: I cannot be certain for which team he is batting at present, but I fear it may well not be our own.

I should also like to make clear that ███████ is an utter ███. He was recently found in ██████ with ██████ and raspberry-flavoured jelly ice cream on the ████-██████████. The unofficial word is he likes ████████████ and (unusually for someone of his background) Marmite, but only if it is applied to his ████ by a ██████ ██████ while watching TV with a ██████. It is best I feel that I draw a veil over the excessive use of peanut butter on the ████. Or indeed the ████████.

While our own dear Prime Minister is known to ██████████ with ██████████, it is on nothing like the scale of ██████ seen here. Indeed, it has probably not been witnessed since the days of ██████ and their rampant ████████.

Last night the ██████ was seen departing with ██████ whilst announcing that ██████ was his fantasy idea of ████████. The Russian president, unfortunately present at the same event, was seen to laugh and comment "In my country, we say a ██████ like this is a ████████████." (The translator assures me these are the correct words to use, unlikely as it may be to encounter them in diplomatic circles).

I fear this only serves to prove that the old adage—that in theory there is no difference between theory and practice, while in practice there is—holds sadly true.

We are all ██████—utterly, utterly ██████.

I am, Yours Sincerely, etc., etc.

The Civil Servant

J acky McDaniels was busy in her Whitehall office long before Big Ben bonged seven. It was a well-established daily routine. First in, last out.

At this early hour she was at her most productive, enjoying the tranquillity and opportunity to focus before the bagpiping busker took up position on the corner of Parliament Square, tirelessly tormenting the theme from Braveheart until the fading last light of day.

Calling it her 'office' was a deceptive misnomer. The typical Whitehall workplace has morphed into a confusion of open plan corridors rammed with cluttered desks, dented lockers for personal possessions, lopsided computer screens, misconfigured chairs, tea-stained mugs, rodent traps (mice and rat varieties), the stale sock-and-broccoli malignant odour of yesterday's microwaved lunches and the inevitable debris and detritus created by a workforce destined to scramble every day to find somewhere half-decent to sit and work.

Even when a seat can be found—invariably broken, maladjusted, labelled proprietorially, or just plain wonky or dangerous—working amidst the noise and chatter and general ambience of a rush hour train carriage was hardly conducive to thoughtful, creative or productive activities. Yet the cult of open plan has become an unchallenged theocratic doctrine of Whitehall's 'New Public Management', besotted as they are with metrics and tick boxes, formulaic processes and a worship of presenteeism over outcomes.

The custom of empowering civil servants to take the time to focus on quality has all too-often atrophied into a competitive mad race to 'just get it done', spurred on by the never ending carnival of Ministerial musical chairs— with most Ministers seldom in position long enough to understand their brief, let alone deliver anything of significance.

Despite these challenges, McDaniels remained dedicated to doing the right thing, especially for her staff. She'd initiated the welcome institution of providing Krispy Kreme doughnuts and handmade gluten-free cakes for her team every Friday morning: a warm, instinctive, and genuine gesture. It wasn't long before her idea was misappropriated however by less well-motivated senior managers, who adopted it solely to veneer themselves as 'people people' in the hope of accelerating their own visibility and careers.

Her first hour at work was occupied with deleting and archiving a deluge of emails—emails that should never have been imagined, let alone written and sent. Emails concerned with attention-seeking, mansplaining and unashamed point-scoring over colleagues rather than solving the complex policy issues facing the department. Yet she felt compelled to read them: every single one. Occasionally there would be the odd flash of light, a rare message of importance or amusement camouflaged amongst the weeds.

Today's batch contained a classic. The Minister was requesting permission for a drinks cabinet to be installed in his office for 'general entertainment purposes', including 'hospitality for visiting dignitaries and officials from within the UK and abroad. And others.'

McDaniels particularly admired that suitably vague, catch-all addition: 'And others'. It was a topic about which the Minister was evidently passionate and knowledgeable. As well as specifications for the cabinet itself—

```
Solid wood, I suggest a mahogany or oak, rather than
cheap veneer. We need to reflect the values we stand
for. And lead crystal drinking vessels rather than
cheap mass market stuff.
```

—there was also a list of proposed contents. It included the finest spirits to ever bless a drinks cabinet, with numerous 50-year-old whiskies the Minister was reportedly particularly familiar with. On a frequent basis. Priceless whiskies that she would be happy to sample herself, should the occasion ever arise.

There was little reason for the Minister's proposed indulgence to be refused. Drinks cabinets were once commonplace, if not *de rigeur*, amongst both Ministers and senior officials. The all-important 'precedent' had long since been established, even if more recently it had fallen out of favour amongst the New Management puritans. Besides, McDaniels welcomed the idea. It would reintroduce a small splash of colour into a Whitehall increasingly corseted by conformity, groupthink and risk aversion.

She forwarded the Minister's note onto the Permanent Secretary's office with a recommendation the request be quietly approved.

Another more notable email outlined the provisional answer to a Parliamentary Question. She knew the MP responsible for its submission: he routinely queried the department, although his PQs were rarely, if ever, his own work. They were usually drafted for him by curious constituents, nosy old-school journalists, or companies seeking information for commercial advantage. The department's proposed response to his latest query was an exemplary masterpiece of evasion and meaninglessness, a semantic black hole devoid of content.

She considered the worthless draft reply, wrestling with the rebellious idea of following her instincts and answering the PQ honestly and comprehensively. It was the right thing to do, even if her political overlords, and most of her fellow senior civil servants, would disapprove.

There was a popular and admirable phrase that the inrush of digital insurgents to Whitehall had incanted as part of their new religion: '*Make things open, it makes things better.*' This near-revolutionary and naïve heresy had long since been stamped upon and crushed of course by the established Whitehall priesthood, but she remained quietly and rebelliously sympathetic to its intent.

McDaniels felt it her civic duty as a public official in a democracy to be as open and honest and kind as possible. Such oddly unfashionable characteristics were partly why progress in her career was proving much slower than it should have been for someone of her ability. Her belief that it was better to work quietly in the service of others rather than to expect recognition or reward rubbed rudely against the ascendency of the self-promotional spirit of a growing cadre of ambitious Whitehall officials, busy claiming personal credit for the work of others.

McDaniels routinely found herself placed in the 'wrong' section of the civil service nine-box talent grid, a management stack-ranking mechanism integral to the oxymoron of the 'Talent Toolkit' and designed to screen out anyone remotely challenging to Whitehall's embedded culture and orthodoxies.

The toolkit achieved its intended purpose with admirable success, ensuring that only self-similar people with the 'right attitude' failed upwards to the most senior levels. It artfully reinforced the practice of 'guided distribution', whereby line managers puffed and promoted themselves and their identikit chums at the expense of anyone perceived as being remotely disruptive, or indeed genuinely talented. The toolkit invariably frustrated her desire to appropriately recognise her own team and their performance, particularly those unique and gifted individuals who had most to offer, but fell outside the accepted 'norms'.

Given the many internal systems, people and processes stacked against her, it often surprised McDaniels that she'd progressed as far as she had—a progression attributable solely to a handful of exceptional Ministers, and not the broken school of management by tick-box. But good, supportive Ministers had become a rare and endangered species.

She reworked the reply to the PQ, sharpening and improving it without making it *too* informative—otherwise the re-written text would be heavily pruned and censored by the department, anxious to prevent any useful insights leaking into the public domain.

How much easier life would be if all Whitehall information and papers were published automatically and promptly by default and only sensitive papers held back by exception, she thought. Citizens deserved to know what happened in their name. But reversing the prevailing ethos of an entrenched bureaucracy, from self-serving and inwardly focused to public-serving and externally focused, was about as likely as a Minister putting their hand up and resigning voluntarily at the first hint of sleaze, scandal or disgrace.

It was little surprise that a former Prime Minister regarded his biggest regret as opening up Whitehall through the Freedom of Information Act:

```
You    idiot.   You   naive,  foolish,  irresponsible
nincompoop.   There   is   really   no   description   of
```

```
stupidity, no matter how vivid, that is adequate. I
quake at the imbecility of it.
```

She finished answering the PQ. It was now honest, factual and useful—
and therefore unlikely to survive intact. But at least her conscience was clear:
she'd done the right thing, unwelcome as that might be.

As quickly as McDaniels emptied her inbox, more emails appeared. The
dressing-gown prima donnas were logged-in early today, slurping their milky
teas and coffees at home while busy generating and dispatching '*Look at me—
I'm online!*' messages before showering, dressing and heading into the office.
Few had any thought for the depressing consequences their endless digital
presenteeism had upon their hapless recipients.

The Ministerial special advisers—Spads—were no exception. A more
misnamed group would be hard to conceive. Their impressively
encyclopaedic lack of knowledge left them ill-placed to advise on anything,
least of all to contribute something 'special'. Who in their right mind, she
wondered, would appoint as their adviser someone whose only experience of
life was attending a major public school, studying politics, philosophy and
economics at university and (at best) working briefly for an MP as a research
assistant?

McDaniels checked the time. In twenty minutes she'd be meeting with
the principal Spad, a government party loyalist who'd padded obediently
along behind the same Minister as he ascended slowly through various
Whitehall portfolios. Neither the Minister nor his Spad understood anything
about their previous departmental briefs, and even less about their current
one. But the Prime Minister found the Minister a vital member of his Cabinet:
he was a remarkably effective political bad news magnet, able to attract into
his orbit whatever cock-up or disaster happened to afflict the government.
He provided an essential media shield for the Prime Minister, usefully
distracting everyone from his own habitual ineptitude.

She re-read the two page briefing note she'd sent to the Minister the week
before. It followed the prescribed formula: a one line summary of the Issue;
a few paragraphs of Background and Issues arising; possible Options; and a
Recommendation. At the end it included a few notes on 'PR Lines to Take'
and 'Manifesto Alignment'.

The template was strictly enforced, including the requirement that no
pictures or images be used—even when they'd provide a far more effective
means of communicating complex issues to a busy and easily distracted

Minister than truncated, cryptic text.

The Minister's office, or more accurately the Spad, wasn't happy with the brief. It contradicted an important element of the government's much-trumpeted, but little implemented, 'Mega Green Dream'—a series of endless and regularly repeated official announcements on the environment that had contributed more hot air and gasses than they would ever remove.

The impending meeting concerned so-called 'Super Meters'. The concept was admirable: to provide fancy new digital electricity and gas meters to better inform consumers of their energy usage and hence reduce energy consumption. However, the policy exhibited one small, tiny weeny defect: it achieved nothing of the kind. Instead, it added substantial hidden charges to consumers' energy bills while having a negligible impact on consumption—least of all for those in fuel poverty and unable to pay higher charges. It had spawned a cottage industry of incompatible meters that locked consumers into current suppliers and left the energy grid vulnerable to cyberattacks. Other than that, it was going entirely to plan.

The programme should long ago have been cancelled, but it was caught in the habitual 'too big to fail' Whitehall Catch-22—a victim of the egos, impossible Ministerial promises, vested big industry and lobby group interests, and billions of mystical 'sunk costs' involved. And so it carried limping onwards, sucking in ever more money and producing the very opposite outcome of that originally promised. It provided yet another case book example of the fate of every vainglorious government initiative predicated on dogma and 'political intuition' rather than evidence and social impact.

McDaniels was diligent in her preparation for the meeting, despite knowing it would serve no purpose. She laboriously assembled and reviewed years of evidence and research, going back through the long sad history of the Super Meters programme and its many Ministers and so-called Senior Responsible Owners.

As she closed her laptop and headed towards the staircase, she knew that facts and rational arguments would count for nothing. It was only the Spad she was meeting, not a subject matter expert with an objective interest in the subject—it would be all about the PR 'optics', the perception and politics of the programme, not the inconvenient truths. The policy's original objectives had long since been forgotten.

She made a silent bet with herself about how long into their meeting it would be before the Spad arbitrarily and smugly set aside her arguments and evidence, as he habitually did, and then uttered his favourite vacuous and utterly meaningless catchword—'Forwards!'

Ten minutes she decided. Yes, ten minutes before the Spad theatrically announced his decision—a decision doubtless taken long before the meeting took place. If she was wrong, and reached the fifteen minute point before that happened, she would count the meeting a great success and the highlight of her day.

Or more likely, the highlight of her week.

The Chief Operating Officer

G ary Bunter, Chief Operating Officer of Mañana International, loathed 10 Downing Street with an uncontainable and seething passion. It was a loathing that festered and engorged with each visit to the official home of the British Prime Minister.

He found the Downing Street residence a broody and depressing edifice of pre-Dickensian greyness and squalor, the moth-balled and decaying relic of a one-time imperial greatness long since departed. It provided the most eloquent rationale for why Bunter's ancestors had fled Westwards from the rotting, gas-emitting, and distended carcass that was the UK to harass and evict Native Americans from their lands and restart life in the 'new' world.

Bunter took his place at the head of the Mañana International delegation as it was guided up the Downing Street staircase past the miserable staring faces of former Prime Ministers. He attempted to appear interested in his host's tedious ramblings about the blandest and least consequential figures he'd ever encountered.

"Blah, blah, first female prime minister, blah, blah, greatest hour, blah, blah, blah, gormless two-eyed git, blah, blah, acclaimed international war criminal, blah, blah, blah."

The voice of the Number 10 lackey droned and swarmed around him like an irritating, buzzing insect. Bunter smiled politely if unconvincingly, masking his inner anger and desire to lash out and squash the source of his annoyance into silence.

The Mañana entourage were ushered into a musty smelling room dominated by a large walnut table—a beautiful, purloined antique from the era when the UK had romped, pillaged and subjugated people merrily across the planet.

Various senior figures were seated along one side of the table and looked up briefly as the Mañana team entered.

"Ah, Mr Bunter," the Prime Minister intoned, extending a hand of greeting and using one of those polite British phrases which meant the very opposite of what it appeared to indicate: "How marvellous to see you again."

"Yeah, whatever." Bunter wondered if the Prime Minister's youthful companions were on day release from a local elementary school. They looked all of eight years old and, unless he was hallucinating, dressed in shorts, dainty ankle socks and sandals. One of them had even dispensed with shoes and socks entirely and sat at the table barefoot and cross-legged stroking his prepubescent attempt at a beard. "Thanks for taking the time to see us."

"Oh, not at all, not at all. My pleasure." The Prime Minister gestured to Bunter and his entourage to be seated. "Tea? Coffee? Hobnob?"

"Coke please. Full fat. None of that zero-calorie shit," Bunter responded, shuddering at the thought of either of the proposed beverages. British tea? Nothing but lukewarm drain-water wrung from week-old dishcloths. And British coffee? Indeterminate grey granules of uncertain origin, an offence against every international treaty concerning biological and chemical warfare.

His attention was caught by the Apple iPad on the table in front of the Prime Minister. *Apple!* The sight of the fruitily named appliance made him want to retch and vomit. For a moment he came close to reaching out and throwing the vile gadget across the room at the juvenile special advisers with their blow-dried Tintin-esque fuck-quiffs. But he held himself in restraint, surprised with the ease at which he exerted Zen-like self-control at a moment of such provocation and duress.

Instead, he reached into his bag and pulled out an oversize slipcase containing the latest world-beating innovation from his own company, a Mañana XXXX-2020 World Edition™. The XXXX-2020 World Edition™ was a stroke of genius, a slim touch-sensitive tablet running the same software as the world-famous operating system that powered the majority of computers on the planet. Mañana's Global Worldwide Marketing Envisager, Minky Tinky, and her team of User Experience Analyticologists, had evolved the uniquely catchy name after tireless months of focus groups, user research, A/B testing, internal debate and the toss of a coin.

"Prime Minister, we have a terrible problem."

"Oh gosh. Do we?" The Prime Minister looked up from his iPad for a moment with the slightest hint of contrived concern.

"Yessah!" Bunter thumped the table, rattling the teacups. "China."

"China? Oh, I do apologise. I was under the impression you Americans preferred to drink directly from the can?"

"No, no! Not china the crockery, China the country! With a capital C for Communist Crooks! Thieves and pirates, the lot of them," blustered Bunter. "They steal and duplicate our excellent software and never pay for it! It's an outrage, a violation of every human right known to, well, known to mankind."

"Oh, how so frightfully annoying for you." The Prime Minister's low-key response was disappointing, his attention apparently focused instead on his iPad and pressing matters of state. From this angle, however, Bunter thought it looked suspiciously as if the Prime Minister was playing Clash of Clans.

"The Chinese communists are ripping off our intellectual property! They are shameless rogues and charlatans! Bolshevik bounders! Marxist marauders!"

Bunter raised his voice, hoping his message, repeated with sufficient force and invective—and a trace of involuntarily projected spittle—would penetrate the Prime Minister's studied indifference.

"Take a look at this. I have the statistics, the degenerate scorecard of international grand larceny, to show you."

Bunter pressed the recessed and elegantly illuminated power switch on his XXXX-2020 World Edition™. A moment passed. Nothing. He pressed it again. The screen stayed resolutely dark.

"Is there a problem?" the Prime Minister enquired, swiping through several colourful and highly responsive screens on his iPad.

"Cocksucker!" shouted Bunter, perhaps a little too loudly.

There was a sharp intake of breath from the Prime Minister and his advisers.

"Not YOU cocksuckers, THIS fucking cocksucker!" shouted Bunter, throwing his XXXX-2020 World Edition™ angrily at the floor, fracturing the SupaStrength™ screen.

Someone was going to pay for this when he got back to the States. Someone was going to pay BIG TIME. Fuckers!

The Cybersecurity Spy

Maximillian Pucker was a contradiction—a spy with a high public profile, the UK media's go-to PR-friendly spook. A veteran maestro of easily digested, snack-sized soundbites, Pucker was frequently called upon to write articles about cybersecurity in language simple enough for even an MP or mainstream journalist to understand—no mean feat.

It would take a dedicated and very lengthy search of news websites to locate any articles about cybersecurity that did *not* include a quote from Pucker, since they are all equally infected with his contributions:

```
Max Pucker, a government cybersecurity specialist
said: "This is potentially the largest incident I'm
aware of. It's big. On a bigness scale from 1 to
10, it's nearly a 9."
```

And:

```
Government    cybersecurity    expert    Mr    Pucker
commented: "This could be a huge story, if it turns
out to be significant."
```

And:

```
"These types of state-sponsored hacks are all about
one side doing something the other side doesn't
expect," explained world-renowned cybersecurity
specialist Maximillian Pucker. "About getting what
we call 'advantage'. Tilting the table. Milking the
herd. Tugging the goat. Loading the die. Gaining
the upper hand. Think of it as an international
game of three-dimensional digital virtual chess.
Played at warp speed. It's crime Jim, but not as we
know it."
```

Pucker spent most of his life presenting slides on the conference circuit, selflessly sharing his expertise and insight into sensitive issues of national security. The fact that many of these apparently 'sensitive' issues were already to be found extensively documented on Wikipedia, for those who had the inclination to look, had done little to repress his enthusiasm or inhibit his career. Indeed, without Wikipedia it is doubtful whether Pucker would have had a career at all.

When he was not enlightening the media or performing on a public platform, Pucker maintained his high visibility with those who mattered by pacing the many corridors of Whitehall and Westminster, popping up unannounced in random meetings and making good use of his 'access all areas' cybersecurity pass. He much preferred the offices of political power to his parent agency's mothership, the large cowpat-shaped building near Cheltenham. His day was more likely to be spent hobnobbing with Permanent Secretaries, Ministers and big technology suppliers than it was huddled in his agency's small outpost nearby, discreetly located above a celebrated vintage comics and porn shop.

This week was not turning out to be an agreeable experience for Pucker. His advice on a matter of great importance had been causing unforeseen political fallout. Even the Prime Minister himself—*the Prime Minister!*—was now reported to be unhappy, his chances of getting a new Bill through Parliament torpedoed by the poor quality of technical insight from Pucker.

It was an unfortunate turn of events. Pucker's career had previously been blessed with luck. His advice was never normally questioned—testament to how few people around him understood technology, and least of all anything bearing the mysterious label 'cybersecurity'.

It was so long since Pucker was last questioned in any detail about his technical advice that he'd overlooked the rather inconvenient truth that he understood nothing of any consequence about technology or how it worked. For most of his working life this had mattered little. Whitehall and Westminster were world renowned—even celebrated in books—for harbouring an eclectic mix of philosophy, politics and economics bluffers and tyre kickers. As a result, it was somewhere he'd always felt entirely at home, able to offer his advice without any fear of challenge or expert contradiction.

He pondered his options over a cup of reliably indifferent coffee in the 100 Parliament Street deli. Where had things gone wrong? It had seemed blindingly obvious to him that the high-tech company Mwahahaha-Wahei, despite being a plaything of the Chinese Communist Party, should be allowed to help upgrade the UK's national telecommunications infrastructure. Otherwise, the country would fall even further behind in the great digital space race. He had argued persuasively that Mwahahaha-Wahei and its genocidal communist paymasters could be kept out of anything sensitive—kept out of the critical 'core' of the telecoms network as Pucker liked to describe it—and hence they could enjoy the best of both worlds: access to advanced technology heavily subsidised by the ambitious Chinese state whilst ensuring that the UK's security and resilience were not undermined. It was, he had confidently assured everyone and anyone who mattered in Whitehall and Westminster, a 'classic—capital W—Win-Win'.

Pucker's advice had subsequently been robustly and rudely challenged, in both the House of Commons and in the trade press. 'Digital Tech Weekly', that relentless, ankle-biting scourge of Whitehall and technology malfeasance, had even dared to point out to its readers that there was in fact no such thing as a 'core' network. This irresponsible disclosure had proved a life-changing event for Pucker. It was one of the rare occasions when the relevant Wikipedia entries had badly let him down, leaving him helplessly and hopelessly exposed.

Now Pucker was facing all manner of difficult questions. Not only from Whitehall and Westminster, but also across the whole gamut of social media from people who knew what they were talking about—including several acerbic computer scientists from Cambridge who were implying that he was little more than a hollow PR shill for his employers in the West Country. Worse, those very same employers, far from backing him up as he had expected, were outraged when they learned of Pucker's advice. It contradicted their expert knowledge of Mwahahaha-Wahei's insecure technology—technology that allegedly leaked everything and anything that passed through it back to its Communist mothership paymasters (although whether by design or technical incompetence remained a moot point).

Most of his career, Pucker had basked in the warm praise associated with his easy-to-read blogs, articles, interviews and flowing (and frequently whimsical) conference speeches. The real problem with his advice on Mwahahaha-Wahei was that he'd broken his own guiding principle: never, on any account whatsoever, provide a simple, straightforward or binary answer. In breaking that doctrine, in providing understandable, actionable 'Yes' or 'No' type advice—rather than advice which could merely be 'weighed up' and 'considered' and 'debated', 'pondered' and 'reflected upon'—he'd fallen into a trap he'd long sought to avoid.

It was Pucker's worst mistake since using a whiteboard to share Top Secret information during a confidential briefing in Downing Street. At the conclusion of the meeting, he'd discovered to his horror that the pen was clearly marked 'Flipboard use only. Indelible ink. NOT FOR WHITEBOARD USE.' With the assistance of a colleague, he'd hurriedly unscrewed the compromising whiteboard from the briefing room wall using his trusty Swiss army penknife. Safely cloaked beneath their coats, they smuggled it pushmi-pullyu like from the building via the internal corridors of 70 Whitehall and into the back of a cab. The embarrassing whiteboard was later ceremoniously incinerated, and the ashes provided to Pucker in a small golden urn as a keepsake, in what he assumed was intended to be a humorous gesture.

Cybersecurity—including the whispered threat of the mysterious and dastardly 'Dark Web'—was one aspect of technology that even the generalists of the civil service took seriously. The fear and apprehension the term caused had enabled Pucker to involve himself with anything that took his interest, to dabble a little bit here, a little bit there. And until now it had all been a game, a quite harmless game.

Pucker switched on his ultra-secure laptop. The tedious wait while it fired up, downloaded and installed updates, rebooted, updated, rebooted, bluescreened—*Kerching!*—rebooted and finally let him log in using a combination of his user ID, password, fingerprint, strangely forgettable memorable fact, and two-factor authentication courtesy of a random one-time number generated on his secure if obsolete Canadian phone, seemed more drawn out than usual.

Finally he was ready to start researching his detailed response, the unquestionable rebuttal that would enable him to set aside current doubts about his advice and settle back into the more comfortable routine with which he was long familiar.

He launched what had been the industry's default state of the art browser a decade ago and navigated to Wikipedia.

'Now I will show them!', he thought to himself, jabbing with his left and right forefingers until the lengthy entry for 'Cybersecurity' was displayed.

It was time to start editing. If there had been no 'core' to the UK telecoms network before, there soon would be. Pucker, aka occasional Wikipedia editor 'CyberMeister101', was about to make sure of that.

The Stationary Stationery Spider

The stationary stationery spider waits. And waits. Eyes deep set, dark and unblinking, her greying hair sideways combed. Patience is needed. Sometimes nothing falls into her web for days, even weeks. So many years has she watched and waited, motionless in her Whitehall institutional lair, that she has long since lost track of time and the reality of the world outside.

But wait! What is this?

The spider detects unauthorised movement near the stationery supplies and scuttles in with surprising speed.

"Stop! Stop right there! You! Yes you! What do you think you're doing?"

The victim is caught in the act, one hand in the stationery cupboard, fingers resting incriminatingly on the A5 portfolio notepad (Premier Edition, Ruled).

"I'm sorry? What the—"

"Your pass! Show me your pass. Now!"

The spider scrutinises the proffered staff pass and smiles smugly.

"I knew it. You do not work for us."

"I'm after stationery for a meeting. You know, to take notes."

"Of course you are! That's what they all say!" the spider sneers. "I just need *this*, I just need *that*. I just want *this*, I just want *that*. But this is not YOUR stationery cupboard, is it? This is not your stationery cupboard at all. This stationery cupboard is for HR and Finance and you are from—" She double-checks the pass. "From IT! IT! Disgusting!" There is pure outrage in the spider's querulous voice.

"None of this stationery is for you, nor shall it ever be. This is HR and Finance stationery for HR and Finance people. And possibly Official Visitors invited by the most senior of senior management. But only if and when I say so."

"Oh, come on now, be reasonable. We all work for the same department."

The spider shakes her jowly, grey head. She has heard every excuse, every snivelling, grovelling *'But I'm special!'* pathetic plea before.

"This is OUR cupboard, not yours. Stationery for HR and Finance, not stationery for IT. Be gone! Get ye to your own stationery cupboard, digital Beelzebub!"

For a moment her victim is tempted to seize the A5 portfolio notepad (Premier Edition, Ruled) anyway and stick two fingers up at the spider. But the spider moves with a surprising burst of speed to close the door, leaving the victim a brief moment to snatch her hand clear before the metal slams shut.

The victim sighs with frustration and a hint of anger.

"Oh for fucks sake! Are you fucking insane?"

And then she is gone, stomping angrily away in defeat.

The spider smiles and retreats to her seat.

Where she can watch.

And wait.

The Futurist

Penistone Smallwood was well-established around Westminster and Whitehall as the 'go to' futurist, keynote speaker and influencer—roles he had shamelessly promoted over many years and to many successive credulous governments, Parliaments and corporate clients.

The surprisingly poor track record of his self-professed 'expert insights' and 'near and far' future prognostications had done surprisingly little to stall or deflect his career. His nickname of 'Dodo'—naturally never uttered directly to his face (although sometimes muttered *sotto voce* in his presence after a long evening's drinking)—provided a harsh, if fair, assessment of the true value of his lacklustre, and surprisingly expensive, predictions. Smallwood remained blissfully unaware that the only reason most companies eagerly used him was not for his prophetic acumen, but to exploit his ludicrous fees in order to run up a loss for tax purposes.

Today he was busy updating his personal website:

"Penistone Smallwood, adaptive futurist (near and far), philosopher, keynote speaker, No.1 influencer, digital whisperer, visiting professor. Transforming FUTURE tech into NOW tech."

Smallwood had been momentarily delayed with this important task after inexplicably locking himself out of his account. Once the problem was resolved—he had foolishly misread a capital O as a zero while copying his universal user ID and password from the sun-faded sticky note adorning his monitor—he started to tap on his keyboard, one careful prod of his right index finger after another.

Such was Smallwood's assumed familiarity with his chosen topics that he never lost precious time on the much-overrated concept of 'research'. He was proud to expend minimal effort slavishly keeping up with the latest geeky trends and fashions, as so many lesser so-called 'futurists' did. To do so, he sniffed, would merely make him yet another mindless victim of groupthink and confirmation bias. Far better to remain aloof from whatever latest fad was enjoying its ephemeral moment of glory if he were to provide value to those who treasured his opinions and insights. In any case, he found it much easier to wait and see what his second-rate 'competitors' were writing and tweeting about, and then skilfully repackage their ideas into something more erudite and perceptive.

"The future is what we make it."

Yes, he thought, nodding to himself. He liked that as a title. He liked it very much indeed. In one short, pithy phrase it encapsulated one of his most profound and original philosophical insights. But first he needed to provide sufficient context to make it intelligible to the lay reader.

He resumed his stabby, stubby finger-poking abuse of the keyboard.

"As I explained to the Prime Minister at one of my exclusive Downing Street insight and foresight briefings, the future is what we make it. He was delighted with this revelatory insight. Yet without the temporal intuition that I and I alone can bring, very few of our leaders understand this fundamental truth and hence their own cognitive risks.

"I'm reminded of the time when a former Prime Minister—now rendered notorious and discredited in certain circles due to vainglorious misadventures overseas—wanted my guidance on his ideas for harnessing the power of new technology—'neo-tech' as I have both minted and coined it—in the National

Health Service.

"I was flattered by the invitation and provided him with useful and insightful advice in return. I understand the NHS has never been quite the same since—high praise indeed. Of course, if I knew then what I know now about him, I'm not certain I would have agreed. In particular, it's a matter of shocking regret that a senior politician expected my guidance and insights to be provided free of charge, rather than in return for the usual pecuniary arrangements to which I'm so well accustomed. Still, an important lesson learned as they say!"

He paused to laugh in ritual appreciation of his wit. And then he resumed his laboured keyboard prodding—short, erratic bursts of activity timed to coincide with the rise and fall of his excessively obese and highly regarded stomach.

"We must strive towards a wholeness in oneself, towards personal mastery of both our minds and bodies, as I once instructed two of my most personable and capable international students—Muammar and Saddam—before they sadly and mysteriously lost their way. I have struggled to understand what went adrift there. I taught them everything I know and they always paid my invoices promptly too. In cash—US dollars as it happens, a most agreeable currency. Such a terrible loss.

"No matter. One must not look backwards, for there lies the past, but forwards, where I believe the future can be found. Indeed, I was conversing recently with one of the world's so-called leading experts on Darwinism and evolutionary theory. Naturally, I pointed out several egregious errors in his much-acclaimed popular and best-selling 'thinking', particularly in relation to anthropological trends and the emergence of what I call 'Homo Technologis'— the technologically augmented poly-modal self—in place of 'Homo Sapiens'. Yet he looked at me as if he'd never heard of any such thing and called me an 'anchor' or something similar. Well, flatter me as he might, I found his lack of knowledge unbelievable. Clearly he'd read neither my books nor articles, and was all the poorer intellectually for it.

"It is a matter of personal regret that I frequently encounter similarly disadvantaged individuals, self-deprived of my unique and generous interconnected insights. I refer to them as the 'fractional people'—the *fracti-populi* as I detail in my many articles—since they are not all there. Parts are missing, as it were. Parts that can only be refreshed by drinking at the ejaculating fountain of my seminal knowledge.

"Such *fracti-populi* are only one third, or perhaps three-eighths, present in a world where wholeness, represented by the Number 1, or unity, is needed. They are the Humpty Dumpty people—fallen and broken into pieces—when what we really need is a world of wholeness. To be whole is to be complete, which coincidentally happens to be the title of my first highly successful book.

"We were once promised our future world would provide us with a luxurious life, one where computers liberate us to enjoy endless idle days of plenty and leisure. Technology will free us, they said, taking on all the tedious mundane and unrewarding work, leaving mankind and womankind and childkind free to exploit their full potential. A sort of modern luxury techno-Communism as some have provocatively dared to position it—albeit one assumes without the mass executions, wars, genocides, industrial failures, gulags, misery, food shortages, slavery, torture, brutality, coups and wanton bloodshed of course.

"Well, we know how that amateurishly optimistic prediction of a life of leisure turned out, don't we? My new playbook, '*The future is mine—and possibly yours*', is far more accurate and reliable. £50 hardback, £30 paperback. Smallwood Transcendental Press. All profits to the author. It builds on my recent successful tomes, '*The 7 tribes of personkind*' and '*Why Me-Time follows Tea-Time*'.

"Encapsulated within my broader thesis is the realisation that technology will enable the emergence of the all-caring state. This emotionally engaged state will nurture us as a mother (or other non-gender-specific parenting persona) does a child. We shall soon enter the world of 'Future State', one that requires us to wear caring technology, something I have termed 'Careable Technology' or more simply 'Careables' (international trademarks pending).

"Careables will soon lovingly embrace and augment us, as the comforting womb of womankind (or other womb-facilitated persona) embraces the unborn child during pregnancy. Though I confidently predict this breakthrough technology will be with us far longer than nine months of course.

"We are living in a remarkable, digital age, an era I like to call the 'omni-channel post-industrial world'. I am often asked my secret to how we can thrive in such times. I cannot summarise easily. These are complex matters that only a privileged few of us are able to understand, so you'll need to reserve a place on my introductory five-day bonding and fondling course. But in essence we can compost ourselves and bloom into flower through the rigorous and selfless application of my patented Four Step Plan:

Step 1. Make a List.
Step 2. Do the things on the List.
Step 3. Remove the things you have done on the List.
Step 4. Go to Step 1.

(All rights reserved. ©Penistone Smallwood. International Patents applied for)

"This approach builds on and updates my earlier, but slightly less comprehensive, Three Step Plan. One of my most able and accomplished alumni, Austin Dumper, probably the UK's leading Chief Procurement Manager (I'm sure you will have heard of him), has used it successfully to build and enhance his career and reputation.

"It represents centuries of wisdom that I have refined and redefined for our modern age, reducing the cognitive overload that threatens, like a tsunami, to overwhelm us, and decluttering one's soul through the principles of my patented Smallwood's Feng Shui LiteBite—bringing everything into harmony. And all at a very reasonable introductory price too.

"This all forms part of my homeopathic practices for survival in the modern world, although complete mastery requires a minimum ten-day residential course. During this time, we spend two days on each of my Life Steps, from decomposing what it means to both 'List' (as a noun embracing connectivity and wholeness) and 'List' (as a verb, the work of composing the records and creation of the artefact, recognising the temporal resonances of indicative present, indicative present continuous and infinitive present), and the remaining days in collective meditation and worshipful contemplation of the List, and indeed my bill.

"Paper and pens not supplied."

Smallwood stopped, and reviewed his work with immeasurable pleasure. What inspired form he was on today. Time for a camomile tea, he thought. To be followed by the treat of a rooibos-infused colonic irrigation.

"What a time to be alive!" he smiled to himself. "What a time indeed!"

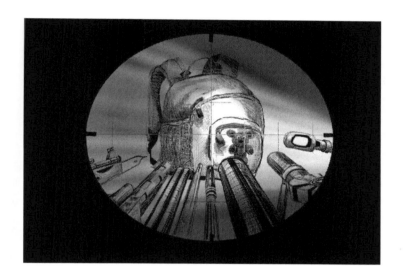

Scuttle's Speech (Part 1)

Edwin Scuttle was in a good mood—a noteworthy and exceptional event. The cause of his jubilation was simple: formal confirmation of his long-overdue promotion. He was no longer Director General of Internal Security (Designate) but Director General of Internal Security (Absolute).

It provided a welcome vindication of his selfless and public-spirited programme of attrition, humiliation, intimidation and indeed outright bullying of politicians, civil servants and the media. And much more importantly, it provided a renewed opportunity to shine a bright light on the difficulties facing his personal lifetime crusade, the War Against Terror (WAT).

Until now his mission had been undermined by one particularly irritating and insoluble problem: the British people were simply not fearful enough. He struggled at times to understand them. However great the terrorist

63

outrages he helped cultivate, the general public remained uncowed, nonchalantly going about their daily lives, enjoying themselves and invoking a maddening nostalgia for a mythical Blitz spirit, ignoring the occasional slick, and sick, video rant from one blood-curdling medieval re-enactment extremist or another somewhere in the world. Instead they preferred to indulge themselves in sharing videos of kittens meowing Christmas songs and generally looking cute—and, of course, getting hopelessly, brain-numbingly bladdered (the public that is, not their cats).

This was a total disaster that he had not originally foreseen. Without widespread Fear and Trepidation (FAT) about the Fear of Terrorism (FOT) the government was in danger of losing the WAT. People urgently needed to be much more frightened, worried and intimidated—to be quite literally 'Terrorised'. The FAT and FOT were essential if the WAT was ever to succeed. He had even drawn it in large letters on the simplistic Hostile Secretary's whiteboard:

$$FAT + FOT = WAT$$

And underlined it twice. In red. And then stood over the Hostile Secretary while she wrote it out 100 times in her Hostile Office branded notebook. How much simpler could he make it for her? Otherwise his whole cunning plan—to oversee the implementation of internal security controls for the greater good—was in danger of never gaining credibility or popular acceptance.

Scuttle sat at his desk and reviewed the press coverage of his recent speech. It was the first of several beautifully conceived events designed to turn the population away from their complacency and into a state of abject fear and trepidation. As a result, the long-awaited Fear of Terrorism would soon be recultivated, at which point his draconian, illiberal draft legislation would pass easily through the Houses of Parliament, with MPs and Peers once again willing and naïve bleating lambs to the slaughter.

Ah, here was what he had been looking for. Toadying coverage of his recent speech, perfectly positioned on the websites and front pages of the compliant and ever-predictable media:

```
Backpack manufacturers have become "command-and-
control networks for terrorists and criminals", the
Director General of Internal Security at the Hostile
```

Office has said.

Terrorist extremists had "embraced" the use of backpacks, but some companies remained "in denial" over the problem, Edwin Scuttle said in a speech delivered today at the Bognor International Gala for Bigging-Up Total Terrorism (BIGBUTT).

He called for them to do more to co-operate with security services.

However, civil liberties campaigners said the backpacking companies were already working with the intelligence agencies. None of the major backpack manufacturers has yet responded to Mr Scuttle's comments.

Mr Scuttle went on to say that terrorists had "embraced the use of backpacks as a transportation channel via which to carry materials that promote themselves, intimidate people, and radicalise new recruits."

The "security of backpacks" added another challenge to counter-terrorism initiatives, he said — claiming that techniques that relied on "solid fabrics" being used for the backpacks (a technique known in spy craft circles as "hiding the contents in the bag") had "once been the preserve of the most sophisticated backpackers, but they now come as standard".

GCHQ and its sister agencies could not tackle these challenges "at scale" without greater support from the private sector, including the largest US backpack companies which dominate professional hiking, he said.

Mr Scuttle stated: "They [backpack companies] aspire to be neutral conduits of stuff carried around on people's backs and to sit outside or above politics.

"But increasingly their backpacks not only carry the latest Primus stove and Up-In-One™ tents from camping stores, but the material of violent extremism or child exploitation and provide for the facilitation of crime and terrorism.

"However much they may dislike it, they have become the command-and-control networks of choice for terrorists and criminals, who find their backpacks as handy as the rest of us."

The challenge was to come up with "better arrangements for facilitating lawful investigation by security and law enforcement agencies than we have now", he said.

The debate about whether security agencies should be allowed to access the contents of backpacks was brought to the fore after a whistle-blower leaked details of alleged mass backpack surveillance by US intelligence and GCHQ — known as "taking a cheeky peek" in intelligence jargon.

Earlier in the year, an investigation revealed how terrorists were using popular backpacks — including ones used for "tourist piss-ups" to Bournemouth — to boost the popularity of their material.

"What we need the backpack manufacturers to do is 'man up', and ensure that in future all backpacks are made using completely transparent material so that we can see what's in them whenever and wherever we need".

Scuttle was delighted. It gave him even more joy than his promotion. If he could maintain this level of sycophantic coverage and momentum, public opinion would soon reject the wishy-washy liberal elite and—more importantly—the much-overrated concept of democracy itself. At last FAT, FOT and WAT would turn in his favour. Britain and its errant adult children were about to finally fall into line with his plans.

Time for another sherry.

The Insecurity Minister

Dame Barquing-Dogge, government Minister for Insecurity and Intrusion, enjoyed speaking at large, corporate events. Today she was excited to be keynoting one of the most significant and highly regarded professional security conferences on the UK circuit. Only those with the highest levels of government clearance—the mysterious SC or DV, embellished by something called a 'strap'—were invited to attend.

She walked up to the lectern, determined to make an impact.

"Thank you, Chairperson. Good morning and welcome. What a privilege it is for you to be here today, to hear first-hand about the increasingly complex nature of national security and indeed cybersecurity.

"I do not pretend to be an expert on every possible cobwebby nook and cranny of these intricate topics, particularly in company as distinguished and niche as this. After all, one does not know what one does not know. The future's not ours to see, whatever will be will be.

"Nobody can claim to know all the necessary hashtags. This reality, this 'truth' as I call it, is a major consideration in the way we, in government, are updating the national security strategy. We shall bring it into full digital alignment with the Fourth Industrial Revolution. In so doing, we shall defend our assets, deter our adversaries and prescribe a new and effective cyber hygiene throughout the nation, from the largest corporations to the humblest citizen. I shall be taking on board your feedback today. These hands are listening, I can guarantee you that."

She paused, holding her hands aloft for dramatic visual emphasis.

"You may not have seen it, but I have. Over there. Look. Do you see it?"

There was silence in the conference centre. Excellent. She knew she had their full attention.

"I call it the 'elephant in the room'. And what a big, grey elephant it is, with very large ears. African I think rather than Indian."

She waited a moment in anticipation of a reaction—a collective gasp of admiration from her adoring audience, or perhaps a rippling Mexican wave of sage nods of approval regarding the wisdom of her insight. And once again, she was disappointed. What a curiously poor calibre audience, she thought. Clearly they hadn't consumed sufficient caffeine at their mid-morning break. No matter. Her dramatic and compelling call to arms would awaken even the most somnambulant cyber anorak.

"There is much of importance to be discussed. Security, or as we like to flatter it in this age of the interwebs, cybersecurity. And data. Small and big data alike. We do not discriminate. The internet of thingamajigs. Bits and bytes. Big, complex issues like this. These are the elephant, or rather elephants, to which I refer.

"We must face hard truths. The world we knew yesterday is different from the world of today. And different too from the world of tomorrow. It's an ever-changing world. Change changes everything. We must look forwards to where the future lies, not backwards to the past, as the eminent futurist Penistone Smallwood so wisely informs us. The Chinese apparently like to say 'We live in interesting times', but I think it more accurate to say 'We live in interesting times, for the times they are a changing'."

Barquing-Dogge paused. The continued lack of any audience reaction was baffling. A few individuals at the back of the room stood up and drifted out, making energetic and cryptic hand gestures towards her. What was their problem? Not the slightest hint of a laugh, or polite smattering of appreciative applause. Her vital message was evidently going well over their heads, despite their so-called cybersecurity 'expertise'. She would make a point of talking more slowly and more loudly to aid their comprehension.

After an early promising start, national cybersecurity was proving a disappointing, poisoned chalice. No, not just a single poisoned chalice. A whole series of toxic drinking vessels lined up along a bar stretching to infinity and beyond. There were times when she regretted ever agreeing to accept the brief. It had started as a jolly good jape, a welcome and high profile opportunity to help the UK become a more secure, digital by default nation. The role had appealed to both her head and her heart: who could resist or stand idly by when your country so clearly needed you?

In opposition she'd excelled in the role, ceaselessly mocking and taunting the government, calling out their inconsistent and shambolic proposals. It was a gratifyingly simple task, facilitated by the limitless help and expertise readily available to any opposition political party. Barquing-Dogge tapped repeatedly into the insights of a large and supportive group of talented, knowledgeable people—academics, civil society specialists, former security insiders, and the big, household names of the technology industry.

Drawing on their advice and guidance, she soon made a name for herself, establishing a reputation as a formidable expert and repeatedly tripping up and ridiculing the hapless government, exposing errors and weaknesses in its so-called thinking. Her opinion pieces filled the columns of leading newspapers and magazines, and her television appearances saw her frequently demolish her ill-prepared political opponents.

The unexpected success of her party in the subsequent general election had changed everything—and not for the better. The moment she stepped inside her Ministerial office, she found herself rudely excommunicated from her external sources of expertise. The self-professed cybersecurity 'knowledge' of her new Hostile Office team was a travesty of the in-depth advice and insight she needed: she became an actor without a script.

Her team of freshly assembled officials had arrived hotfoot and enthusiastic from a random assortment of Whitehall departments, bringing with them their recently acquired knowledge of national standards for pelagic fish filleting, preferred methods for streamlining the workbasket of communications enquiries for junior Ministerial correspondence, and overseeing the optimal design of export declaration forms for high vegetable content, hazelnut-infused chocolate snacks. They were all, the Permanent

Secretary assured her, in the 'correct', high-flying part of the civil service 'Talent Toolkit' and hence accomplished at communicating and influencing, seeing the big picture and delivering at pace. Although precisely what pace no-one could tell her.

After working with her for several months on security policy, and just when she felt they were finally becoming useful, they would disappear to assume new-found expertise in other departments—helping deter welfare claimants, optimise the offshore tax system for global corporations, devise farmers' subsidies on skylark landing strips, or plan anti-immigration policy.

Disillusioned and unable to access her former expert advisers, she struggled to retain her motivation and credibility. Even the counsel of the Chief Scientific Adviser to the Hostile Office, the impressive Professor Polly Quibble, had proved largely irrelevant on the topic of cybersecurity, although Barquing-Dogge now possessed an expert in-depth knowledge of the science and realities of global climate change.

She now understood why it had been so easy in opposition for her to outshine the previous government. Its Ministers had been caught in the exact same trap as herself, cast adrift from the expertise and advice needed to fulfil their roles. Now the tables were turned. Free to draw upon the wellsprings of expertise that forged her own reputation, the shadow spokespeople started to undermine and outperform her, chipping away at her credibility. She looked ill-informed and out of touch, exhibiting all the same errors and weaknesses and inconsistencies as the government she'd once so frequently mocked.

She became conscious she'd hesitated, lost in her thoughts. She coughed politely and resumed her speech, trusting no-one had noticed. They weren't exactly the sharpest or most alert of audiences after all.

"The internet has become an open highway for criminals. It's horses for courses. We need to tame and control it, for obvious security reasons. On the one hand, we must tackle the growth of crime and terrorism that lurks on 'The Dark Web', whatever that is. On the other, we must preserve our democratic values. And we cannot tackle these problems with one hand tied behind our backs. We must untie our hands and recognise that the so-called defenders of 'privacy', whatever that may be, have become shameless apologists for evil.

"We need to confront and tackle these difficult problems, not merely wring our hands and witter on about 'civil liberties' or 'human rights' or other 'do-goody' virtue-signalling things. We must resolve these complex problems calmly, recognising they represent opportunities and challenges. I may not have a degree in technology, but I've always found in politics that one does not need to understand everything. Or indeed, anything. Too much knowledge is a dangerous thing. It's basic common sense we require. Where would we be in a world run solely by 'experts'? Who needs them?"

She laughed, the only sound in the hushed hall of experts.

"Now, what you must understand—and I say this with reasonable confidence and authority—is that the future may take one of several different forms. But to be prepared is to be prepared, as I often remind my Whitehall team. And I have to say, regardless of their many other failings, my officials are superlative at drafting things, at craftsman-like wordsmithing and producing copious documents and charts and graphs that I can print out and discuss with my opposite numbers in the European Union, the United States and elsewhere. Indeed, this is the approach I have championed with the Five Eyes alliance—although to be frank amongst friends, it's time to open all of our eyes. The *Ten* Eyes alliance, that is what we need. We and our allies should certainly not be looking around the world with one of our eyes closed, for obvious security reasons.

"And this is why we're investing substantially in cybersecurity. Millions and millions of Treasury funding in fact. We shall bring a bright shining torch of truth and justice to bear on the darkest illicit corners of 'The Dark Web'. Where there was darkness, I say let there be light."

Barquing-Dogge waited in anticipation of warm applause, applause that never came. This was becoming tiresome. Even her staff were not responding appreciatively at the right moments, despite knowing precisely where pauses for applause were highlighted in the speech. Inexcusable—they'd written it for her, incorporating essential insights from Edwin Scuttle, the highly regarded Director General of Internal Security at the Hostile Office, and one of the few Whitehall insiders with an expert and vicelike grip of the subject.

She looked around, missing the days when her appearances had been greeted with enthusiasm and popular acclaim. Was it her imagination, or was the room emptier than when she'd first taken her place at the lectern? There was the distinct and growing buzz and hubbub of lively conversation, and possibly even laughter, coming from the adjoining coffee lounge.

"Successful national security requires eternal vigilance," she resumed, talking more loudly to ensure she could be heard. "Not only to protect us against the dark handiwork of criminals, but to enable us to track and understand the scale of the problem.

"Government and our trusted outsourced surveillance capitalism partners already monitor every single communication and activity that citizens do online. Now the same approach is required inside organisations too. If you don't know what your employees are doing and thinking every minute of every day, you're not doing your job properly.

"Consider it as a form of collective insurance, a warm, much-loved comfort blanket—the emergence of the 'protective state', as my delightful colleague Mr Scuttle has characterised it. He is, as those of you who know him I'm sure will agree, one of our truly good people. His vision is of a benevolent, ubiquitous state that looks after us, even before we know we need looking after. A state that understands and tracks everything, which sees into every corner of our lives in order to keep us safe and secure in our beds at night, caring for us from the cradle to the grave.

"Where the Chinese Communist state leads, and I think it does so with great inspiration and necessarily ruthless innovation in this particular area, we in the West will doubtless follow. People are very happy to do so with the large social media companies, living their lives in the loving embrace of corporate intrusion and surveillance. Now is the time for government to get in on the act too, to stop outsourcing this important responsibility to the private sector and to bring it in-house, as it were.

"This is why I'm so excited about our Interception of Private Life (Citizens) Bill. My officials have worked very closely with the technology industry and other governments. We've consulted widely, and I acknowledge the admirable assistance received from varied and surprising partners, including the Russian, Chinese and, indeed, the North Korean governments. They're very good at these things, I'm told by Mr Scuttle—international exemplars that we lag far behind.

"Bring your so-called enemies and their ideas close as they say, for obvious security reasons. We should not be proud in such matters, these are difficult times. Technology is a complex thing, and we need to learn from who we can, where we can, without fear, favour or prejudice.

"So let me finish my speech here today by making it absolutely clear that we shall do whatever it takes to remain at the cybersecurity vanguard of the digital revolution. Of that, you have my word."

Barquing-Dogge hesitated momentarily for dramatic impact, and then raised her arms aloft and shouted enthusiastically at the top of her voice:

"*Viva la revolution!*"

After which she made a dramatic, low bow and waited for the rapturous applause indicated in her script.

And waited.

The Activist

Derek Wormbore rated himself highly. And it had become his custom—even something of a ritual—to do so publicly, frequently and loudly.

He was, at least by his own account, the UK's most effective and feared civil society activist. Clever enough and shrewd enough to perceive things that others did not, to speak truth to power where others would not dare. It was a skill that only he truly understood and appreciated—a skill that made him such a dazzling activist, with a loyal and surprisingly high Twitter following.

Wormbore spent much of his time diligently unearthing political subterfuge. Deep, dark-state subterfuge that only he was sufficiently talented enough to perceive. And joining up conspiratorial dots, however random those dots might appear to anyone less gifted.

He often wondered if he were the only person on the entire planet able to spot the dots to be joined up. Spotting and joining up dots, even invisible and non-existent ones, was what he did—with great accomplishment. It led him to all manner of startling discoveries and conclusions about the real intent of Machiavellian government policy—policy against which he would then loudly activate his activism.

Wormbore assumed that the frequency with which he was 'let go' from endless contracts and advisory roles by civil society organisations was the inevitable by-product of gratuitous envy of his own brilliance. He saw it as further confirmatory evidence of his deliberate marginalisation and oppression by those whose his rare intelligence and insight threatened.

The mundane reality observed by the people who encountered him was that he was overly prickly and difficult to get on with. His highly rated and loudly proclaimed intelligence was in fact highly rated only by himself, and his sense of humour lacked, well, humour leading him to often entirely miss the point of a joke. Yet the absence of any sense of personal self-awareness or humility meant that he remained oblivious to these less than appealing behaviours.

His most recognisable character trait however was his habit of interrupting whoever was talking—and in particular women—in order to finish their sentences for them (unfailingly wrongly), or to fundamentally misinterpret the point they were making in order to showcase his innate male grasp of the topic at hand.

Today, listening to the directionless chatter of the meeting around him, it was clear to Wormbore that once again his insightful observations were needed to save the day.

"I think," Wormbore stated, learning forward on the table to make his point and interrupting the Co-Chair as she was highlighting an important issue. "That the Minister will need to reconsider this aspect of the Bill. It needs a rethink."

The group momentarily looked at Wormbore, checked he'd finished and then returned to their deliberations. The conversation resumed for barely a second or two before he interrupted again.

"I think," he stated, learning forward on the table to make his point. "That the Minister will need to reconsider this aspect of the Bill. It needs a rethink."

The group hesitated. Had there been a Groundhog-Day style time warp resulting in Wormbore contributing the same thought over and over again?

A few members looked at the Co-Chair for guidance. She shuffled the agenda and attempted to pick up the threads of their discussion.

"So, if we—" was as far as the Co-Chair got.

"I think," Wormbore stated, learning forward on the table to make his point. "That the Minister will need to reconsider this aspect of the Bill. It needs a rethink."

Wormbore couldn't believe it. How many times would he have to repeat and labour his sharp insight and astute contribution to the lacklustre meeting before the group understood? Were they as STUPID and as SLOOOOOOW as they seemed?

There was no helping some people. But he would not become dispirited. No. He would merely repeat his observation as many times as necessary until it received due recognition.

In behaviour reminiscent of a young child, whenever Wormbore made a contribution of which he was particularly proud, he would echo it tirelessly until fulsome praise was heaped upon him. His tweets were in a similar vein: he would tweet and retweet and quote tweet his insipid and second-hand insights until the number of 'likes' reached his required minimum vanity threshold.

Unfortunately, Wormbore's 'insights' were rarely, if ever, anything like as perceptive or useful as the outbursts of a young child. For this reason, lavish praise or indeed faint praise, was rarely generated in his direction. Which only compounded the problem.

"I'm conscious of time. We really must—"

Wormbore cut in before the Co-Chair had completed her sentence. "I think that the Minister will need to reconsider this aspect of the Bill. It needs a rethink."

The group was frozen. Clearly it would be up to Wormbore to hand hold them. He could barely contain his anger at being the only one present at the meeting who understood the situation and yet—once again!—he knew it would be him—alone!—left to save the day.

"Look," he continued, talking more loudly and slowly to help them better understand as he pulled a crumpled note from his pocket. "I've drafted an exemplary letter to the Minister that I'm prepared to donate to the group, even though I acknowledge the unlikelihood of you understanding it. It's been carefully crafted to bring the Minister on board and get her to accept our points."

"Oh, really? Have you?" the Co-Chair enquired, failing to keep the scepticism, and a hint of loathing, from her voice.

"Yes. Let me read it to you," said Wormbore:

"'*Dear Minister. Your lacklustre performance notwithstanding, your failed approach modernisation of the necessary strategy shambles. As result neglect, it beholden to I to instead remedy shortcomings.*'"

Wormbore paused. "Obviously, we can change 'I' to 'we' when we send this letter from the group, I'm prepared to let you do that. I'd like to make that clear."

There was silence.

Wormbore sensed that he now had their undivided attention.

"'*Your insane desire drive on with this shoddy piece of work typical of poor performance of both yourself and your inexperienced officials. All along department has petty, dismissive, arrogant and stupid. You failed listen to my insights and special knowledge time and again. A grave error.*'"

He stopped. "Obviously, we can change 'my' to 'our' when we send this letter. I'd like to make that clear."

Encouraged by the continuing silence from the group, which he interpreted as a sign of shock and awe and possibly even near religious rapture at his insights, Wormbore moved quickly on.

"'*Your actions have destroyed integrity of the government and what stands for. How many bad ideas is possible to flowing from a single departments.*'"

Wormbore looked up. "That is what I call a *rhetorical question* for your information, assuming you know what that is of course, which seems unlikely."

And then resumed:

"'*If you are make progress, a bad idea needs replaced by good idea. Or indeed bad ideas by gooder ideas.*'"

"That is my—'our'—gooder idea, I'd like to make that clear.

"'*If you to make progress, then you need listen me*'—'us'—'*and move on from doom-mongering and coercive practices. I*'—'we'—'*therefore look forward meet with you and officials so show right forwards.*'"

"There," Wormbore said, sitting back smugly and looking pleased with himself. Once again he had saved the day. "That should do it. All perfectly clear, perfectly reasonable and perfectly argued. So much better than anything else I've heard here today. What do you think?"

There was a long and uncomfortable silence.

"Which Bill do you think we're talking about?" the Co-Chair enquired.

Wormbore snorted. "What? Really? That's obvious. This one. Doh!"

He waved a crumpled copy of a Parliamentary Bill entitled 'Rodent Habitation Regulations (Westminster and Environs)'.

The Co-Chair looked down at the 'Interception of Private Life (Citizens)' Bill that she and the others had been diligently working their way through for several hours, and silently held it up to display its cover.

Wormbore stared, unconvinced and unrelenting. So the dots had not led him where he'd anticipated. Not yet anyhow. But he knew they would do so eventually, given sufficient time. His instincts were never wrong. This was precisely the type of theatrical subterfuge and deception that he'd come to expect. He knew better than to be downhearted or distracted, unlike the hapless and gullible groupthink victims gathered around the table. More fool them.

He sat back and smiled knowingly. His time would come, he was sure of it—he could see it foretold in the dots.

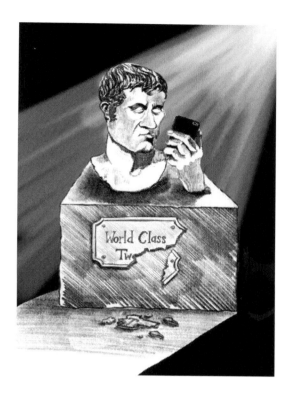

The Super Angel

M ilo Gruntz Caracaras Junior checked his Twitter account, eager to discover how many additional supplicants he'd acquired in the last twenty-four hours. He was disappointed, remaining stuck at well under half a million adherents—an embarrassingly low number for someone of his international status and pre-eminence.

Still, sheer numbers weren't everything, where they? Quality over quantity. At least his followers were smart. Smart enough to like and retweet his daily dew drops of wisdom—the informative insights acquired from his unique, serial start-up career and technology industry nous. But surely there must be *way* more than a paltry half million of them? His so-called rivals had Twitter followings that were significant multiples of his own.

He shook his head, bemused. What was he doing wrong? He had an official Blue Tick to signify his standing as a globally recognised leader—a maven even—in his field. Through his trailblazing blog posts and articles, through the admirable superciliousness with which he treated everyone around him, and through the sheer déjà vu familiarity that characterised his tweets, considerably more followers should be flocking to learn from his sermons, to retweet and quote tweet and idolise his every ingenious utterance in adulation.

It was he, Milo Gruntz Caracaras—*the* Milo Gruntz Caracaras no less—who had hewn, chiselled and shaped Silicon Valley long before the concept even existed. Or at least, that was the reputation he sought to establish for himself, constructing a successful revisionist narrative that he'd single-handedly created one ground-breaking West coast technology company after another. And while none of his companies were successful in that rather traditional and boring old-fashioned business sense—such as turning a profit or surviving more than a few years without either imploding with massive debts or being devoured by a competitor—that was not the point.

Caracaras's well-crafted media persona positioned him as a pioneering serial entrepreneur brimming with transcendent ideas. Despite his litany of failure, he was very rich and highly sought after. His opinions were quoted repeatedly and widely on the internet, and echoed mechanically and uncritically in mainstream media, business and government. He'd become an annual Esteemed Guest of Honour at the World Technology Forum (WTF) in Sovad, the legendary media circus where the most prominent politicians, technologists and dilettantes came together to burnish their egos, promote their latest ghost-written books, and decide how to reshape everything to their own mutual advantage, boorishly talking great power and privilege to democracy and truth.

It was in Caracaras's likeness that the West coast tech world had been so successfully moulded and exported across the planet. An image he characterised as innovative, entrepreneurial and ground-breaking, unlike his critics—who sneeringly dismissed him as obese, balding, middle-aged, male, spoilt, shallow, opinionated, privileged, avaricious, condescending and blinkered, to name but a few of their more favourable assessments. Caracaras blithely acknowledged the inevitability of great leaders provoking strong negative reactions—what was it Shakespeare said? '*O beware, my lord, of jealousy; It is the green-eyed monster which doth mock the meat it feeds on.*'

Well, his critics could rant as much as they liked. It didn't matter. The world-leading influence of West coast technology was his doing. It said so on his website. Which, had it been true, might at least have explained why the internet had drifted so far away from its original admirable intent to improve the world into a brash, shallow, misogynistic, racist, bullying, spiteful, surveillance-driven and fact-lite monster manipulated by privileged tech-bros, tax-avoiding corporations and rogue nation states alike. In so doing, it had become a perfect mirror of the values that lay at the heart of Caracaras himself.

"No pain, no gain!" he muttered, typing 'Go swivel!' in reply to an emotional Tweet-storm from one of the sad-heads who endlessly called out what they termed his 'narcissistic privileged white male misogyny', but which he preferred to think of as the trail-blazing pioneer spirit, the gung-ho thrusting, testicular-fuelled masculinity that had forged America.

His critics were easy to dismiss—they were an inferior breed, jealous of his wealth and success. Envious of his undisputed role as 'The New Digital Messiah', as the discerning technology publication 'Blue Tick International'—in which he coincidentally happened to be the major investor—had insightfully called him. It was his critics, and not he, who had the problem. He was a Super Angel Investor. The term 'Angel' reassured him. It told him he was on the side of goodness and light and progress: he was one of the good people.

Caracaras was proud to follow in the pioneering footsteps of the towering business philanthropists who preceded him, the inspirational and benevolent barons and tycoons who'd envisioned and constructed the vital modernising infrastructure of their own age, the railroads and oil industry. There was always collateral damage in the process of change, those who would be trampled underfoot, hurt and left behind. But America would never have been built at all if it weren't for his own kind seeing and seizing and shaping the future. Every generation needed its pioneers, its visionaries, its Caracaras.

Perhaps his greatest achievement of all however was to have promoted himself as the creator of the exciting and revolutionary concept known as the 'digital calendar'. This self-proclaimed breakthrough enabled him to schedule his time, allocating every activity to a precise hour each day. Or even, incredibly, its organisation by the minute—catering for essential aspects of his inspiring routine such as '07:30 wake up', '07:35 floss', '07:40 shit.'

It was—as he was fond of telling everyone—a digital revolution in time and space, enabling him to bring structure and sequencing into his frenetic life. The 'calendar' was the program for his own existence, the successive sequence of steps that set out what he would do each day, what he needed to achieve, the scheduled encounters with others keen to meet and learn from him. The routine it provided had not only changed his own world, but now—courtesy of his latest syndicated articles and Angel investments—was shaping the world around him too. But perhaps his most transcendent idea of all was the complementary concept of the 'Weekend'. Days set aside for what he termed, 'downtime and upgrades.'

'Weekends will rebuild the world!' he mused aloud.

The unregulated, free-floating, Zen-like 'Weekend' was the perfect counter to the structured work ethic of the 'Week'. The conceptual brilliance of the calendar—*his* calendar—had spread across the globe, even winning a WTF Ingenious Genius Award the previous year in Sovad. He'd declared it to be the biggest advance of the digital age, the inclusion of every single event that happened in his life in one place.

Many of the 'breakthrough' ideas he evangelised so passionately and profitably may indeed have already existed beforehand, as his crazed, green-eyed, dribbling and drooling critics were quick to point out. But it was he, him, Caracaras, the Super Angel, who realised and articulated their significance. As a result, he'd been showered with recognition and awards, including his appointment not only to the Global Technology Leaders Panel advising the US President, but also that of the British Prime Minister. Caracaras had become a familiar figure in the corridors of power in Washington and London and beyond, helping lead and guide the digital revolution in public services with predictable consequences.

A recent deep data, artificial intelligence-enhanced analysis of his calendar had revealed the startling reality of his life. He wasn't in charge of anyone, didn't produce anything, didn't deliver anything. In fact, he didn't directly *do* anything. That was surely the true wonder of the digital age. It left a maven such as Caracaras free to focus on what mattered—to devote his time to Twitter and other social media, to promote himself while humiliating and vanquishing his critics, to publish ghost-written articles, and to take part in scripted advertorial interviews to enhance his unique global brand. Then there was the occasional investment—*Angel* investment—where he blew excessive amounts of money naïvely entrusted to him by rookie venture capitalists who thought they were backing the Next Big Thing.

Caracaras considered himself the ideal Super Angel to advise investors, CEOs of international corporations and world leaders precisely *because* he was unencumbered by the superfluous experience of running an organisation of any size, had never managed people or delivered products, and possessed zero acquaintance with investing money successfully.

His own technology start-ups either burnt through investors' money quicker than a wood burner through petrol-infused logs; exploded like a defective counterfeit firework, showering flaming remnants on anyone and everyone in the vicinity; or were acquired by a rival business after they'd swallowed the hype about the 'advanced technology' Caracaras claimed to be developing. Such acquisitions were invariably subject to protracted legal action and expensive out-of-court settlements.

He read carefully through the draft of his latest article, authored by one of his most reliable and best paid scribes. It was a characteristically self-deprecating piece about his mind-blowing innovations and how they were leading and reshaping the world, reforging it in his own image. High technology was the planet's newest and most influential religion, complete with its evangelists, social media pulpits, angel investors and West coast priesthood. It was therefore no surprise that he'd been anointed as its only true prophet, the new Digital Messiah—and not solely because he'd paid good money for the privilege.

Caracaras now aspired to distil his world-influencing insights into something that less intelligent, less capable followers could understand— accessible articles and blog posts and tweets that would result in ever increasing clicks and hence credibility and advertising revenue. And, most importantly, something that would help nourish and grow his Twitter fan base well beyond its current half million up into the stellar stratosphere of the really big social media giants.

"Praise be to me and all who believe in me," he intoned to himself, sitting back and closing his eyes for five minutes of what his calendar assured him would be high quality 'me time'—a description his critics might well have applied to his entire vacuous existence.

The River

We built this city, murmurs the Thames

    Quietly lamenting its lost sisters and brothers

        They who once played and entwined together where

            Freshwater tastes salt

Great rivers built this city

    Conversed in this once warm valley

        Singing tales of time and journeys taken

            Great rivers this wild landscape

                Cut, forged and

                Tamed

Fleet
    Tyburn
        Walbrook
            Westbourne
                Bollo Brook
            Neckinger
        Effra
      Falconbrook
    Ravensbourne
Brent

Tributaries, backwaters and waterways
    Culverted and veiled from sight
        Running amongst Bodica's ash legacy and
            Skeletons of sharks, crocodiles and wolves

Stand silently beside the Thames and
    Harken its history
        Sonic imprints of the past which
            Whisper and echo below
                Long, liquid memories now
                    Misdirected, pipe-prisoner trickles
                  Where great torrents once
                Flowed

Stand silently beside the Thames and
    Sense the ageless living library —
        Church bells and
            Birdsong, the
                Brush of leaves
                  Travelled through time from
                Centuries ago

Our smartphone, satellite maps deceive

    Obscuring older human records of place, a

        Mudlarked lost landscape beneath

            Every old London map, a

                Revelation, a

                    Layer of ages past and vanished

                        Thorney Island, foundation of Westminster

                        Foundation of

                        Power

On storm rich days the neglected subterranean arteries

    Pour torrent-full, revive the hidden city pulse

        Fluid burst their imprisonment to embrace again the

            Great Thames

                Joyous siblings united once more —

                    Singing yet their tales of time and

                      Journeys taken, and nurturing still the

                    City

                      They

                        Built

The Permanent Secretary

The Minister for Technology was late. Cyrus Leach, Permanent Secretary for Digital Things, was not impressed. His time was important. He had little patience for politicians who didn't demonstrate due deference and respect. If the simple task of time management was beyond a politician, how capable were they likely to be at the rather more important task of managing the country?

Twelve minutes and thirty three seconds late, the Right Honourable Bacchus Jardine MP entered the room.

Leach made an exaggerated show of looking at his watch.

"Oh, have I kept you waiting?" the Minister inquired in a way that suggested he didn't require an answer, before removing his coat and sitting behind his desk.

"Right. Let's run through our updated strategy. We publish it next week," Jardine continued.

"I'm not happy with it, Minister," Leach observed.

"No? Anything in particular?"

"All of it," Leach continued. "In my many years of experience in big business and running large international organisations, I've never seen anything quite like it."

"That, my dear Cyrus, is precisely the point. And let's face it, your previous career experience is hardly an exemplar that we should seek to emulate."

The remark stung. Leach didn't welcome being reminded of the ignominy of his past. He'd been gliding towards the peak of his career, on the brink of elevation to Chief Executive of Sleazings—one of the UK's oldest and grandest finance houses—when it plunged dramatically into insolvency in a spectacular international disaster. Worse, it was Leach's own high risk, and highly rewarded, toxic investment gambles that had brought about Sleazings' precipitous downfall.

He didn't understand why the Minister kept bringing up the subject, gleefully rubbing salt into an open and obvious wound. What was the demise of an ageing, centuries old institution compared to the importance of his own career? One made mistakes, one learned, and one moved on. Such is life. Only through failure can one learn to succeed—on which basis he now had an unrivalled abundance of experience to ensure his success.

A former Chairman of Sleazings had kindly thrown Leach a lifeline following its collapse. Taking advantage of his insider position as a Non-Executive Director in Whitehall, he'd helped secure Leach his impressive government position. Under the guise of bringing in outside 'professional expertise', the nod-nod, wink-wink old boys' network appointment had taken place without any of the inconvenience of the usual tedious formalities, such as application forms, CVs and interviews.

A gushing press release fanfared Leach's appointment—

```
The Prime Minister said: 'We are taking a moon shot
to reform Whitehall and revitalise the public
sector. Cyrus's highly valued experience of
business and the private sector puts him in the
ideal position to accelerate our programme to make
everything natively digital. That is, digital by
default.'
```

—although it remained somewhat sketchy about precisely which of Leach's previous business experiences were so 'highly valued'. It was notable for example in failing to reference his indelible impact at Sleazings. The accompanying quote from Leach was similarly vague about what his role would entail—

> "I am super-excited to take up this position at the beating heart of government's ambitious programme at this pivotal moment in time. My laser-focused priority will be to build on the exciting existing momentum, to strengthen the withered execution biceps of Whitehall and leverage and embed a sustainable productivity agenda as a world-leading resource not only for now but into the future and beyond."

"Minister," Leach said calmly. "Your ambition to accelerate your radical reforms to Whitehall may seem simple, but I can assure you it's not. Numerous representations have been made to me, including from very big and influential companies, as well as EGO, the esteemed technology trade association, that I've found articulate and persuasive. They highlight severe doubts about the impact of the many changes you've already implemented. Indeed, they bring into question the entire wisdom of your plans, well-intentioned as they may be."

Jardine smiled and leaned back in his chair, putting his hands behind his head.

"Cyrus, Cyrus, Cyrus. You worry far too much. The fact that the big companies and EGO are unhappy, even whispering nonsense in the ear of the Minister for Business, Michael Dimswick, is the very proof I need that we're on the right track. Now is the time to challenge old orthodoxies, to be bold. To escape Stockholm syndrome and the stranglehold of the large technology companies. You must surely understand this, you are our pre-eminent digital man after all!

"We're in the exciting, technologically-dominated twenty-first century and yet Whitehall and our supply base remain locked into a Victorian mindset. This is the moment for us to become more radical, to be agile, flexible and digital by default. We need to improve our use of data, overhaul our productivity and efficiency, and root our political decisions in evidence not anecdote and dogma."

Leach had rarely heard such naïve, dangerous ideas. He hadn't got where he was by being bold or radical. Far from it. And he certainly wasn't going to start now.

"We've become hostage to the global technology companies and bloated systems integrators," the Minister continued. "We've lost control of our own destiny to a powerful oligopoly of complacent suppliers. That's why I've tasked you with taking forward this updated, reinvigorated strategy. To make government services better, our technology cheaper, our processes more transparent, flexible and innovative. It's time to open up opportunities for new suppliers, particularly innovative small and medium size businesses."

"Small and medium size businesses?" Leach queried. He wasn't even sure what they were, or why anyone would want to use them. 'Opening up opportunities' to them sounded about as desirable as cultivating a cockroach infestation in a Michelin-starred kitchen.

"Exactly! You've got it," the Minister responded enthusiastically. "I want you to supercharge my work breaking up big monolithic contracts, disaggregating complex programmes and ensuring we have an open and competitive marketplace that ends once and for all the stranglehold of the supply-base oligopoly. Digital is now our default delivery choice, our destiny. This is the future, giving our citizens the services they deserve."

Leach winced.

"We must also accelerate the adoption and use of open source technology and platforms," Jardine continued.

This was beyond bearable. Open source? EGO and Mañana International had warned him of the grave dangers of continuing down that particular Marxist path—in great detail and at great length, courtesy of the outspoken but persuasive Julie Jangles-Daley. She'd come to their meetings armed with endless PowerBore™ decks full of convincing animated facts and figures about the benefits of licensing expensive proprietary products.

"And we shall expand our world-class in-house bespoke development teams alongside taking advantage of the best digital innovation the market can offer."

The Minister was visibly excited. He had no comprehension as he was talking of how much Leach detested it all, the career-challenging, high profile risks his reckless plans represented. There was a good reason Leach preferred simple big fat contracts with big fat suppliers and handing over big fat cheques of other people's money: it outsourced his own risk and responsibility. What the Minister was describing was dangerous. Leach would be taking on personal liability for the biggest shake-up in Whitehall since it started to be professionalised in the nineteenth century. That was certainly not what he'd signed up for.

Leach had been repeatedly assured prior to accepting his inflated salary that he could enjoy an easy few years in Whitehall, make the odd high profile speech, be wined and dined by big corporations, periodically praise the work of officials and suppliers alike, and then receive a knighthood from the automatic gong vending machine. The Minister was in danger of breaking that promise, recklessly navigating him towards dangerous, uncharted and turbulent waters.

"We shall leave no hiding places. Every single bit and byte of government-held data must be made open, exposing waste, inefficiency and duplication across the entire public sector. All expenditure must be published monthly. Citizens have the right to know what we do with their money. Transparency is the key to democratic renewal. Sunlight is the best disinfectant."

Leach's face lost all vestiges of colour. "Publish everything? In the open?" he asked weakly. No wonder the Minister had earned the nickname 'Barmy Bacchy'.

"That's it! You've got it, you've got it! Let's get cracking Cyrus. Light up the bonfire, incinerate the red tape for me. Strip out all the unnecessary regulation preventing our brilliant small businesses joining us. It's time to reinvent and reinvigorate the public sector."

Leach attempted to nod. The Minister was quite clearly mad. Stark, raving mad. Everyone knew that big household brands were the safe choice, not two-people-and-a-dog-in-a-garage type upstarts. It was the very same reason government itself had enormous, monolithic departments offering such impeccable, efficient and streamlined services to the public. Big is Good. Big is Beautiful. Everyone in big business and big government departments knows that. And anyway, a very different kind of revolution would take place if the public ever saw where their money actually went and what they received for it in return. That would turn very ugly and very unpleasant indeed.

Leach's mission was clear. He was going to have to save the Minister from himself and his foolish ideas. It was the decent thing to do. The honourable and gong-worthy thing to do.

Cyrus Leach enjoyed international travel. The limousines, the first class airport lounges, the hotel suites and fine food and wine. Today, his journey was less ambitious—a short-haul business class flight to Frankfurt. The airport was an inspired choice, its hotel and conference centre conveniently integrated within the same complex.

It took just a few minutes for Leach to walk from Arrivals to the hotel and be shown up to his club suite lounge, where a bottle of Krug—a Clos D'Ambonnay no less—was already on ice. The room was modern and light, albeit a little downmarket compared to his usual standards of boutique accommodation. But it would have been churlish to complain given he was travelling courtesy of the generous and benevolent hospitality of McBarnacle and Snatch, one of the finest and most expensive consultancy companies in the world.

Leach placed his suitcase in the bedroom and returned to the lounge where he poured himself a generous first glass. He took a sip and rolled it around his mouth. Ah. Superb. He adored the uniquely exquisite flavour of a Clos D'Ambonnay and sat on the sofa savouring the moment.

His Minister, the Rt Hon Bacchus Jardine MP, knew nothing about his trip. No-one did. It was not in Leach's official diary, and his speech had not been seen let alone cleared in either of Whitehall or Westminster. It was the result of a very special *personal* invitation from the Chief Executive of McBarnacle and Snatch. Few outsiders were privileged to be invited to attend their private, internal company conference.

The entire event was off the record. No reference to it could be found on McBarnacle and Snatch's website. None of its employees would mention the existence of the conference to anyone outside the company, not even to their most generous, loyal and prestigious customers. This was why Leach liked Big Business. He liked the way they thought, the way they worked. Their discretion. He and they understood each other. Intimately.

Leach was privy to important, confidential information. Before leaving London, he received the welcome news he'd long been anticipating. A Cabinet reshuffle was imminent. A reshuffle in which Barmy Bacchy would be removed from office and 'promoted' to the House of Lords. It was a timely tribute to Leach's own fine handiwork. He'd built a resistance coalition of similar minded individuals across Whitehall and Westminster—officials, Perm Secs, MPs and even Ministers, and of course Big Business. The feedback from all of them to Number 10 had been relentlessly critical of Bacchus Jardine:

'Out of his depth', 'Antagonistic', 'Naïve', 'Disruptive', 'Fails to understand Whitehall and the way we work,' 'Confrontational,' 'Anti-big-business', 'Interfering', 'Putting our most important manifesto programmes at risk'. The note from Michael Dimswick, Minister of State for BIB, was particularly scathing and effective—curiously echoing many of the points made by Mañana's Julie Jangles-Daley during their own meetings.

Bacchus Jardine knew nothing of this surreptitious plot of course. But it was for the best. One day the Minister would thank Leach for it. His removal would restore a sense of equilibrium to Whitehall, rolling back all the nonsense about a 'procurement revolution' and 'working in the open'. It was a simple equation. Big departments have big problems and big problems require big solutions and big solutions require big suppliers and big money. The logic was faultless.

Leach was restoring the balance of power to where it rightly belonged. He planned to make Jardine's imminent change of fortune the big reveal of his speech. McBarnacle and Snatch would be the first to hear about it, weeks before anyone else and weeks before it happened. He'd reassure them that the disruptive and profit-damaging changes of recent years would be reversed.

Big business would be back with a bang. Competitive contracts and short-term rolling procurements would be replaced by the highly profitable, escalating price arrangements of the past. Leach would apologise personally for the pain the Minister had caused their business, their lost opportunities, and the diminished revenues and Partner bonuses.

"The good old days are back!" was the defining conclusion of Leach's speech, a punchline calculated to ensure a standing ovation.

With the vocal support of the big departments and big business behind him, the ultimate outcome was in the bag—his knighthood, already pencilled in for the New Year's honours list. As soon as that was secured, Leach would take great pride in leaving Whitehall in a very different shape than when he arrived.

After a suitably discrete interval, he'd accept the very lucrative offer the McBarnacle and Snatch CEO had whispered in his ear over their recent lengthy and convivial dinner at the Holly—and join their Board.

"The good old days are back, indeed," he said quietly to himself, pouring another generous measure of Krug.

Maestro

The Chief Procurement Manager

A ustin Dumper, Chief Procurement Manager, was short. So short in fact that he was often mistaken for a child and locked in the departmental crèche, where he would spend the day having Play-Doh pushed into his ears and nostrils by excited toddlers with paint-stained fingers.

On the rare occasions when Dumper was accidentally allowed out, he'd retreat to his office to totter atop his specially commissioned high-rise stool. It provided the ideal elevation for him to review the gold trophies, rosettes and other assorted procurement industry prizes that lined the room, together with an imposing faux leather, twenty-five volume set of encyclopaedias. But it was the oversized motivational posters of himself that he most enjoyed.

It was hard to know which of these team-inspiring, high-production values photogenic endorsements was his favourite. Riding the winner across the finishing line at the Kentucky Derby? Conducting an orchestra at the Barbican centre? Dancing the leading role in Swan Lake? It was of course a fool's errand attempting to choose between the many similar images staged and paid for from the public purse. They all conveyed him equally well as a Great Leader. Or, in his own mind at least, *The* Great Leader.

Dumper's career had not always been so fruitful and high-flying. On the advice of the school's career service, he'd left full-time education to become a door-to-door encyclopaedia salesman. "People will always need encyclopaedias. You can't go wrong with high-end books," they'd assured him. With impeccably bad timing, he'd taken out a cripplingly large bank loan to fund his new business just as the market imploded. Would-be customers turned to Wikipedia instead, discovering it cost nothing and required zero shelf space. Dumper was left with a lock-up garage rammed to the ceiling with finely bound volumes of the world's most expensive encyclopaedia.

Not one to dwell on his misfortunes, or the dubious wisdom of the school career's advice service, Dumper devoted day and night to reading extensively through every encyclopaedic topic related to contracts and the law. Using his newly acquired knowledge, he soon found new opportunities in business procurement and rose rapidly through his chosen profession, discovering the perfect outlet for his photographic memory and love of wheeler-dealing.

Whenever he settled at his desk alongside the immaculate shrine to his own prodigious achievements, Dumper would summon the department's Public Relations team, keen to monitor the performance of his ghost-written articles and interviews. He was meticulous in maintaining a detailed scorecard of his success, tracking the number of articles published about or 'by' him. He also closely monitored the ceaseless invitations to keynote at conferences and enjoy private complimentary dinners at Michelin starred restaurants— those all-important occasions guaranteed to advance his career.

The comfort and sanctuary of his customised TT RS Roadster with its personalised number plate provided the perfect way for him to travel to the many procurement-related events that cluttered his busy diary. After all, nothing said more about the quality of someone's character, status and commitment to the values of the public sector than arriving at a venue driving a fuel-guzzling, flashy car with a vanity plate.

These high profile outreach activities represented a far better use of Dumper's precious time than tackling the out-of-support and malfunctioning spaghetti of technology in his government department as it lurched from one headline crisis to another. He saw little personal value in becoming bogged down in the problems of his current employer for a very simple reason—he wasn't planning on being around long enough to make any difference.

His career would soon carry him onwards and upwards, well beyond the limited horizons of the department and long before its next inevitable and catastrophic big systems clusterfuck and Public Accounts Committee ritual inquisition. More importantly, moving jobs would enable him to expense yet another set of ageing encyclopaedias to embellish his new office shelves, reducing the dusty backlog that still occupied half a lock-up garage.

Dumper's decision to outsource everything digital or technical to the global systems integrator Roachfungus Glands had been one of Whitehall's most expensive and widely trumpeted deals, even making the front page of 'Government Procurement International'. For Dumper, Roachfungus were the obvious and only choice. They had long been his go-to trusted procurement partner—and not solely because of their generous gift of an historic chateau in France. This thoughtful acknowledgement of their long and mutually rewarding relationship provided somewhere ideal for him to relax and re-charge, despite the unforeseen downside of always encountering hordes of other high-spending procurement specialists curiously resident in the exact same village.

Today was a special day. He was about to be interviewed for a headline article in 'Top Procurement Talent of the World (incorporating 'International Contracting and Outsourcing Today')', the influential and glossy trade journal. He was going to be featured on the front cover in his full air-brushed glory. And not before time, of course.

In his childlike excitement, Dumper cranked his chair rapidly up and down, up and down, up and down. He loved the customised seat. It went far higher than an ordinary office chair, placing him at an extreme elevation relative to visitors occupying the ultra-low, legless seat opposite. Too much of his unfairly vertically-deficient life had been spent looking up at others, but now they were forced to look up to him. All was good with the world.

Dumper zoomed back to floor level and retrieved his luxury, photogenic toupee from the safe—the expensive one kept for *very* special occasions. He combed the exquisite hairpiece reverentially in his hands like a favourite long-haired pet. Once it was finely groomed to his satisfaction, he placed it on his head and adjusted it to what he deemed a suitably raffish, boss-like angle.

Oh yes, this was going to be a special day indeed. Very special.

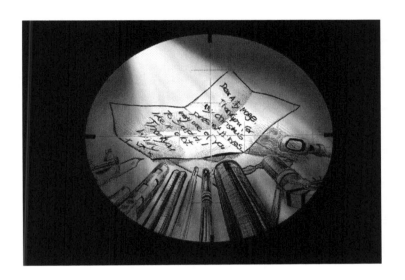

Scuttle's Speech (Part 2)

Stationery manufacturers have become "command-and-control networks for terrorists and criminals", a senior official at the Hostile Office has said.

Terrorist extremists had "embraced" the use of "envelopes and paper", but some companies remained "in denial" over the problem, Edwin Scuttle said in his speech at the Stationery Handling International Tradefair for Bigging-Up Total Terrorism (SHITBUTT).

He called for them to do more to co-operate with security services.

However, civil liberties campaigners said the stationery companies were already working with the intelligence agencies.

None of the major stationery manufacturers has yet

responded to Mr Scuttle's comments.

Mr Scuttle said terrorists had "embraced the use of letters as a transportation channel via which to carry information that promotes themselves, intimidates people, and radicalises new recruits."

The "security of stationery in transit" created another challenge to agencies such as GCHQ, he said — adding that techniques that relied on "envelopes" being used for concealing the contents of communication (known in spy craft circles as "sealed bloody letters") had "once been the preserve of the most sophisticated stationery users, but they now come as standard".

GCHQ and its sister agencies could not tackle these challenges "at scale" without greater support from the private sector, including the largest companies which dominate professional stationery, he wrote.

Mr Scuttle said: "They [stationery companies] aspire to be neutral conduits of information carried around in letters and to sit outside or above politics.

"But increasingly their stationery not only carries the latest update on Aunty Marge or little Willy, but the material of violent extremism or child exploitation and provide for the facilitation of crime and terrorism.

"However much they may dislike it, they have become the command-and-control networks of choice for terrorists and criminals, who find their stationery as handy as the rest of us."

The challenge was to come up with "better arrangements for facilitating lawful investigation by security and law enforcement agencies than we have now", he said.

The debate about whether security agencies should be allowed to access the contents of letters was brought to the fore after a whistle-blower leaked details of alleged mass stationery surveillance by US intelligence and GCHQ — known in tradecraft jargon as "steaming it up 'em".

Earlier in the year, an investigation revealed how terrorists were using popular stationery — including the type used to invite people to weddings, funerals and stag weekends in Slough — to boost the popularity of their material.

"What we need the stationery manufacturers to do is 'man up', and ensure that in future all envelopes and letters are instead replaced by post cards so that we can read the content whenever and wherever we need without having to boil a warehouse of kettles to steam them open".

The Intern

The McBarnacle and Snatch intern flicked eagerly through the draft of the strategy slides she was preparing for Cyrus Leach, Whitehall's Permanent Secretary for Digital Things. She chose a selection of inspiring and relevant material from the seemingly infinite Corporate Doctrine Playbook and remembered to update the title page and footer to reflect the client's name.

"Top and tail without fail," she breathed to herself. There was nothing more embarrassing than presenting a client with an expensive, custom-tweaked deck only to discover the name of a previous customer still embedded within it. A classic rookie error, as she had already learned to her regret. The resulting Partner-led inquiry, salary sanctions and Personal Improvement Plan had fortunately soon put her back on track.

Now that she was a few weeks into her privileged and highly-sought role as an 'Accelerated Diversity Progression' intern—generously offered on the minimum wage for reasons she didn't fully comprehend—she was already familiar with the routine. She would choose and assemble appropriate slides, editing a select handful to provide a hint of content relevant to the client. A Senior Partner would subsequently review them and make at least one spurious change. Then they would be sent to the client alongside a personal note drafted by their Executive Assistant extending an invitation to whatever extravagant corporate hospitality was taking place over the next month or so—golf, Formula 1, hot air ballooning, wine tasting, swingers' party. All of the time and expenses, understandably enough, would be billed at the Senior Partner's rate—reflecting the meritocratic, 'levelling-up' ethos at the generous heart of the company.

The intern double-checked that McBarnacle and Snatch's logo and name—and its rigorously enforced intellectual property rights—were prominently marked on all of the slides. The government might be paying handsomely for the presentation and the thinking embedded within it, but that did not give them the right to re-use or republish it without prior written consent, together with an additional fee in consideration thereof. It was important that clients understood the arrangement was more of a short-term lease than a freehold. They would be privileged to gain world-leading, if expensive, insight, but ownership and copyright would remain at all times with McBarnacle and Snatch. It was one of the finest and most expensive consultancy companies in the world for good reason.

She took her time selecting and re-arranging various topics into the optimal narrative to meet the brief—well over an hour, possibly nearly an hour and a half. Such selfless dedication is precisely why large companies and governments alike utilise highly paid big name consultancies. They do all the hard lifting, sifting through trends and buzz phrases and jargon, distilling Wikipedia entries into expensive, cluttered and often illegible micro-font slides placed into an incomprehensible and meaningless narrative.

The results of her work would provide the strategic arse-covering and senior credibility their client sought, highlighting important and overhyped concepts that only McBarnacle and Snatch claimed to understand. Profitable bingo buzzwords and phrases such as the Fourth Industrial Revolution, Bitcoin, Blockchain, machine learning, artificial intelligence, open data, open standards, agile, entrepreneurial, platform, big data, sustainability, transformation, framework, online, logistics, data-driven, hyper-digital, laser focused, distributed ledgers, digital first, internet of things, data flatulence, digital skills, unlock the value, mission statement, synergistic, scorecard, evidence-based, non-depletable, unleash the potential, priority missions, legacy, opportunity cost, new oil, old oil, ethics, untapped potential, digital twin, systemic, cybersecurity, leveraged, revolution, virtualisation, cloud-first, data scientist, methodology, fuelling growth, productivity, ecosystem and whatever else they could copy from the front pages of the pioneering international business journals and their trail-blazing deep insights into how to make the world a better place—or at least, a more profitable one.

The intern sat back with satisfaction. The slides looked good: smart, slick, boardroom-ripe. A complete strategy ready to roll.

She watched a few of them on auto-play to check the timings worked:

> Our strategy is open. We will lead a secure effort of the market through our use of the internet of things and binary wrench data leadership to build a digital transformation. By being both networked and collaborative, our disruptive approach will drive the culture of a learning organisation throughout the company. Synergies between our insight from data and digital will enable us to capture the upside by becoming agile in a sustainable world. These transformations—combined with our leaders' values—will create a digital business through an updated cultural ecosystem and social media.

> We will lead a sustainable effort of the market through our use of environmentally conscious hyperdigital transformation and data leadership to build a digital business. By being both customer-focused and networked, our secure approach will drive growth throughout the ecosystem and pivot the landscape. Synergies between our big data and customer value proposition will enable us to capture the upside by becoming agile in a digital first, revolutionary world. These transformations combined with design thinking will create an artificial intelligence enhanced big data Blockchain.

> We are an organic, networked organisation. We will envision open and inclusive market research through our use of virtual reality and cultural leadership. By being both innovative and disruptive, our digital first approach will drive the internet of things throughout the echelons of the organisation. Synergies between our artificial intelligence and big data machine learning will enable us to become a cloud-first player operating in a secure world of distributed ledgers. These transformations combined with our world-beating deployment of interactive social engagement will create a truly revolutionary display of bold data platform innovation.

We are in the midst of a digital revolution driven by data. The digital economy is defined by modern technologies and the use of ground-breaking innovations such as artificial intelligence. As part of this fourth industrial revolution, we will ensure that data—in its broadest sense—will lead open and inclusive market research through our use of virtual reality and cultural leadership. By being both innovative and disruptive, our digital first approach will drive the internet of things throughout our organisation and beyond.

Data is a cornerstone of the digital world and a cultural priority for our organisation. It is the enabler of our future business and success, including our transformation into a natively-digital entity. Data is the fuel of our innovation, boosting productivity and positioning our organisation as a forerunner of the next digital wave. We shall lead the way, ensuring that our services are transformed to deliver the best possible outcomes for our users. Our leadership will maximise the differential benefits, embrace the opportunities and unleash the revolutionary power of data to realise the dreams of our users.

She stopped the slides. There was no need to check them all: a random sampling was statistically sufficient. The client would soon let them know if something was amiss. Everything looked good—so good that she decided it was appropriate to prepare the client's pro-forma invoice. £475K + VAT. A very 'special' rate, one reserved exclusively for the public sector. A rate that seemed entirely reasonable, representing as it did several hours not only of her own minimum wage time but also a cursory review and sign-off by a Senior Partner.

It was not so much the *work* the client was paying for, but the *knowledge*, the *value*. And that, as the Senior Partners often reminded her, was nearly worthless. No, no. Not worthless. That wasn't it. What was it they had said? Ah, of course—priceless, priceless.

Nearly priceless.

The Young Hack

B art Malmot was a conviction journalist. Young, ambitious and uncompromising, he considered himself the Hunter S Thompson of Hoxton, the Gonzo of Generation Y, a Bernstein and a Woodward in one slick, street-hip, wordsmithing, spliff-rolling package.

Malmot prided himself on his ability to detect and uncover bullshit, corruption and conspiracy. To expose it in sharply written, cutting-edge, street-savvy prose. Even if—a mere insouciant detail—no such corruption or conspiracy actually existed. Being repeatedly wrong throughout his short but headlining career had proved little obstacle to his self-styled success. It merely confirmed his suspicion that he was the victim of an even bigger and more underhand corporate plot that he had yet to detect and expose.

Today was an auspicious occasion. Malmot had blagged himself a place at the technology industry trade association, EGO, where all the juicy, lucrative and shady deals between Whitehall and the international high tech corporations took place. He had convinced himself that senior government officials were complicit in using EGO to launder their ambitious new multi-million pound programmes, exploiting it as a trusted and non-confrontational environment where a nod-nod was as good as a wink-wink. Talking to one room full of grey-haired grey men in grey suits—and they usually were grey, single-gendered and sartorially similar—ticked all the official boxes of 'extensive consultation' and 'market readiness' without doing either.

EGO had originally been set up as a diversionary piece of theatre by the International Masonic Oligopoly of Big Technology Companies, a useful veneer to mask their stranglehold on highly lucrative public sector contracts. Its meetings were a byword for cronyism, secrecy and intrigue. They were where valuable personal networks and lucrative business agreements were quietly orchestrated behind closed doors in the modern equivalent of the old gentlemen's club. The controlling members of EGO and senior government officials found common purpose in keeping troublesome journalists at a distance. They worried that any exposure of the cosy and mutually beneficial private discussions between Whitehall and big business would not only make them look bad, but prove to be seriously gong-challenging behaviour.

Malmot was a man on a mission. His undercover infiltration of the invitation-only meeting would enable him to expose to the world precisely what went on behind closed doors. He had expertly and brazenly penetrated EGO's inner lair, establishing himself as a cuckoo in its midst. Rather than waiting for a story to come to him, his preference was to force it into the open, assuming his trademark role of journalistic agent provocateur. Malmot had already written most of the ground-breaking story he was about to dramatically uncover. It would save time. Now all he needed was a few random tidbits to fit into his existing, scandalous narrative—select, juicy soundbites that would provide it with colourful and engaging shock and awe.

He stood outside EGO's elegant Westminster head office and enjoyed his morning ritual of a hand-rolled 'herbal' cigarette. It was a moment of calm, tranquillity and introspection before the intense investigative journalism that lay ahead.

As he inhaled deeply, he looked curiously at the luminous, puke green TT RS Roadster with the naff personalised number plate, wondering who it belonged to. Parked directly outside EGO's front door on double yellow lines, Malmot was disappointed to see it had collected only one parking ticket.

What joy it would bring him to see it towed away and crushed.

He stubbed out the remnants of his cigarette butt on the Roadster's front wing, collected his badge at reception and entered EGO's inner sanctum. Achievement unlocked. Although he was openly using his own name, his adopted affiliation was to a non-existent technology company, 'GonzoIT'. The bold cheekiness of it made him smile. And smile and smile. Wow, those 'herbal' cigarettes were good.

Circulating slowly around the breakfast area, he eavesdropped on various conversations amongst the grey suits already assembled. He gorged on a couple of lukewarm bacon rolls, his first real meal of the week, and gulped at the stewed grey coffee, craving the novelty of the caffeine hit. Malmot recognised a few of the portly senior government officials present and the familiar logos of the big technology companies. The usual smattering of smaller suppliers lurked awkward and isolated around the edges of the room, there—as always—to lend the event a veneer of diversity, competition and inclusivity.

"Of course", he overheard one of the fat, jowly suits saying, spraying fragments of croissant and accompanying spittle at his colleague. "This nonsense about disaggregating contracts and using small companies is all very well, but they don't have the experience that we do. You don't employ a small man to do a big man's job. It's all about having the right equipment and length of experience, get my meaning, get my meaning? I can't see this crazy idea lasting. You and me, our companies, we may be big—oh yes!—but we get the job done."

"Too bloody right!" replied his grey-skinned companion, Tweedledum to the other's Tweedledee, and sporting a ghastly mock tartan suit and bright brown shoes. "What sort of idiot would entrust the tax and welfare systems of this country to a smart-arse start-up staffed by hipster youngsters in shorts posting sticky notes on the wall and worshipping bunting and cake?"

"As if they would know what to do, how to deliver big systems! Even if government were stupid enough to give them part of the £20 billion they rightly invest with us. All this 'agile' nonsense, whoever heard of such a thing? What business in their right mind wants to deliver a system on time on budget that actually does what the client wants it to do? One that can be changed easily and cheaply without years of paperwork, change controls and additional payments?"

They both laughed at the absurdity of the idea.

"Where's the fucking money in that Rupert?"

They laughed again, cramming more free food and drink into their mouths.

"Quite frankly, small companies are damned hard work, run by young Turks—idealistic nutters with ambition and a conscience. Seriously, who wants that? It's business we're talking about here, not charity! Using small companies simply doesn't scale. If officials want to sound one of us out, they can pick up the phone, meet us at the club, quaff a few glasses of bubbly in private. But if they need to talk to thousands of teeny weeny businesses, where the hell do they start? They'd have to hire the entire Albert Hall to fit them in! It's too hard."

"Oh, far too hard. And what's the point? It's a splendid embrace of mutual convenience we have with Whitehall."

"That's a nice way of putting it, Rupert. Although perhaps more of a bear hug than an embrace!"

Their ground-breaking repartee caused them to laugh again, spraying yet more flaky croissant down the front of their expensive but curiously tasteless suits and across the floor.

Unknown to Tweedledum and Tweedledee, Malmot was recording their conversation using his expensive and highly prized spy pen. His luck was in. He'd chanced upon the ideal conversation, providing juicy and incriminating quotes that he could weave nearly verbatim into his article. Everything he was hearing merely confirmed his suspicion that attempts to open up government to new, smaller and more innovative players were being deliberately undermined by the old guard, keen to protect their lucrative contracts and their even more lucrative expense accounts and annual bonuses.

Malmot edged closer, nibbling on another bacon roll for cover. He was keen to understand EGO's role in all of this. They had to be complicit, he was sure of it—he'd already said so in his draft exposé. How hard was it for them to invite only smaller, innovative UK companies to turn up and listen to a bunch of Whitehall officials gas on about the latest multi-billion pound technology shambles they had in mind? Why did they still keep inviting the global big tech players into the tent instead? The very same big players that had been helping government technology projects become headline news for decades, one fantastic and mind-boggling disaster after another.

"But let's admit it. Small players can have their uses too, Rupert. It's worth keeping half an ear on what they say. Alongside their crazy, eccentric ideas they sometimes come up with damned interesting insights. Innovative, ground-breaking even, dare I say. Ideas we never would've thought of in a month of canapés. We've won several big government bids by 'adopting' their better ideas and pitching them to our clients."

"And that is precisely why I attend these EGO sessions. You never know what you might learn."

As he finished the bacon roll, Bart Malmot noticed the presence of Austin Dumper, one of Whitehall's highest ranked and biggest spending Chief Procurement Managers. Dumper had been largely invisible in the crowd up until now, with only the odd tell-tale glimpse of his brightly coloured toupee flashing briefly amidst the growing throng of attendees. Now he was heading hurriedly towards the Gents.

Perfect. It was the ideal opportunity to ask him a few questions in private. Malmot sniggered at the thought. 'In private—in the privy!'. God, he was good. He would work a sly reference to that excellent joke into his scoop. His eager-eyed fan would enjoy it.

Malmot grabbed a top-up croissant from a passing server and sidled casually across the crowded room, hoping not to attract attention. He wanted to talk to Dumper alone, without the complication of anyone else joining them in the men's room.

As he pushed open the heavy door to the Gents, he spotted Dumper standing in front of the low urinal at the end. In a calculated breach of the strict and internationally observed rules of male washroom etiquette, Malmot walked over and stood next to him at the immediately adjacent urinal.

"It's Austin Dumper, isn't it?" asked Malmot loudly, unhygienically holding onto his half eaten croissant with one hand as he worked out best how to unzip his fly with the other.

Dumper froze. No-one, but no-one, ever talked to him without a formal introduction and PR minder present. And certainly not in the Gents. This was a disquieting development. He wondered what his mentor, the pre-eminent futurist Penistone Smallwood, would advise in such a situation. Should he make a list?

"Bart Malmot," Malmot continued, slightly muffled as he stuffed the remains of the croissant into his mouth to free up his other hand.

Still Dumper didn't speak. Worse, he was now having difficulty initiating the very biological activity that had been his sole purpose in approaching the urinal. Never before had this important and most sacred of ceremonies been interrupted in this despicably antisocial way.

"Lovely hairpiece by the way," Malmot observed. "You got a merkin to go with that, mate? Matching cuff and collar?"

Dumper maintained an icy vow of silence.

"Anyhow, I wondered how it was going?" resumed Malmot, fiddling energetically with his fly as he spoke. "I see you've got that obscenely big contract coming up for renewal. Project Kronos?"

Dumper was conflicted. He needed to exit the room as quickly as possible, to escape from this peculiar individual who reeked of illegal substances, yet he was also desperate for a wee. If he retreated into the main event now he feared the very real danger of wetting himself. He regretted consuming so many coffees. Coffees that now desperately needed an exit strategy. Yet his system was stuck, shocked into non-productivity by the contemptible and uncalled for breach of every accepted standard of decent urinal propriety. This was close to becoming the worst day of his life.

"The thing is," Malmot continued, finally unzipping his recalcitrant fly and taking the opportunity to relieve himself noisily while he was talking. "I hear Kronos has been a disaster for your department. Millions wasted. Everything delivered late or over budget. I'm very surprised you want to sign up with Roachfungus Glands again. What's the story Austin?"

The informal and familiar use of his first name was jarring. This was beyond awkward. Dumper felt the need to say something, but without his PR minders present he wasn't entirely sure what. He wondered about the efficacy of seeking asylum in one of the cubicles.

He snatched a quick sideways look up at Malmot. It wasn't someone he recognised. Probably one of those eccentric micro business mavericks who needed putting back in their pram. Yes, maybe if he did that this entire situation could be concluded.

"Look," said Dumper, staring rigidly at the sterile white tiles in front of him. "I don't know who you are, but I can tell you this. I will never contract with any silly little company. You're wasting your time. I'm in charge of big complex procurements and big complex contracts and we need big complex suppliers to manage and look after them for us.

"None of that comes cheap. We're in the elite top five of the Whitehall Big Spenders' club for a very good reason, and I intend to keep it that way. I suggest you spend your time talking to the little baby agencies and spurious arm's length bodies. I think you'll find them much more approachable."

With that, Dumper swivelled on the spot, came dangerously close to launching his toupee into flight like some demented furry squirrel, and accelerated into the sanctuary of a cubicle where he slammed and locked the door behind him. A moment later the sound of his urgent, gushing liquid relief echoed around the tiles.

Malmot finished his business at the urinal and shook himself dry. He couldn't believe his luck. He raised his voice above the sound of Dumper's pounding waterfall.

"Can I quote you on that?" he asked. "What you said that is," he added by way of clarification as he zipped up his fly. "Not the sound of you pissing in there. I mean, that would just be silly wouldn't it?"

He laughed. What a most rewarding event this was turning out to be. Today was going to provide the perfect evidence for his scoop. Editors would be frantically outbidding each other for his exclusive, explosive article. But first it was time for another croissant *and* a bacon roll. Maslow's hierarchy of needs and all that.

The Privacy Advocate

Delilah Lox was celebrating her tenth anniversary as Executive Director of Surveillance Resistance Incorporated. Under her inspired leadership, it had been transformed into one of the UK's best-known and most respected civil society groups. It tirelessly investigated government and big business alike, exposing their mutual self-interest in exploiting technology to intrude into and interfere with citizens' personal lives.

Lox picked up her copy of the draft Interception of Private Life (Citizens) Bill. She already loathed everything about it, from its cavalier title to the long, rambling appendix of spurious justifications and explanations, none of which made sense.

"Data includes everything that isn't data", she read aloud from one of its definitions. "What utter bollocks."

She recognised the distinctive hand of the Whitehall official behind it. Edwin Scuttle was a manipulative and toxic Hostile Office Director General from the dark side. He tirelessly promoted his nightmare vision of a 'protective state' where citizens had no secrets and government would act like an overbearing and sanctimonious head teacher, knowing everything everyone did, every second of every day and every night. If anyone had made the lugubrious authoritarian phrase 'Nothing to hide nothing to fear' his own, it was Scuttle. He operated slyly and covertly, undermining, disconcerting and intimidating those who stood in his way.

Lox was well aware of the many subtle and detrimental ways by which society can be corroded from the inside by officials working quietly in the offices of power. While Scuttle's high-profile War Against Terror (WAT) dominated news coverage, it was the covert, drip-by-drip erosion and unpicking of the UK's democracy from the darkest shadows of Whitehall that were proving far more toxic and effective than any overt terrorist action.

She had watched with alarm as a minor change to a rule or regulation here, a tweak of law there, had all tilted the landscape in his favour. It was testimony to the nefarious work of Scuttle and his long-term plan. Much as she loathed him and everything he stood for, she reluctantly admired his ingenuity. He was playing a dangerous but effective game.

This was why the work of Surveillance Resistance Incorporated was so important. It was one of the few organisations fearlessly daring to hold him and his cronies to account, despite the constant pushback and criticisms from Scuttle's attack-dog allies in Westminster and Fleet Street.

She turned to page one of the new draft Bill. Oh. It was bad. Really bad. She reacted instinctively, and loudly, as she read.

"Fuck."

She turned to the second page.

"Fuck fuck."

The third page was little better.

"Fuck fuck fuck."

And as to page four?

"Fuck fuck fuck fuck."

She paused to sip her tea. Darjeeling. This Bill was not looking good. Not good at all. It had Scuttle's oily fingerprints all over it yet again. Time for page five.

"Fuck fuck fuck fuck fuck."

Pages six and seven were not to her liking either. Time for another sip of tea.

"Fuck fuck fuck fuck fuck fuck. Fuck fuck fuck fuck fuck fuck fuck."

She paused. The whole Bill was worse than she had thought possible, an attack on everything that mattered to a civilised society and liberal democracy. It represented Edwin Scuttle at the peak of his dark arts. She quaffed more Darjeeling for reassurance and then turned the page with trepidation to read through the rest of the document.

"Fuck fuck fuck fuck fuck fuck fuck. Fuck fuck fuck fuck fuck fuck fuck fuck fuck fuck fuck fuck fuck fuck fuck fuck fuck fuck fuck fuck fuck fuck fuck fuck fuck fuck. Fuck fuck fuck fuck. Fuck fuck fuck fuck fuck fuck fuck fuck fuck fuck fuck fuck fuck fuck fuck fuck fuck fuck fuck fuck fuck fuck fuck fuck. Fuck fuck fuck fuck. Fuck fuck fuck fuck fuck fuck fuck fuck fuck fuck fuck fuck fuck fuck fuck fuck fuck fuck fuck fuck fuck fuck fuck fuck fuck. Fuck fuck fuck fuck. Fuck fuck fuck fuck fuck fuck fuck fuck fuck fuck fuck fuck fuck fuck fuck fuck fuck fuck fuck fuck fuck fuck fuck fuck fuck. Fuck fuck fuck fuck."

She paused for a moment, suddenly thinking of her kitchen garden.

"Radishes!"

Y

Sir Hugo Montgomery Darcy Bumble exuded the scent of stale smoke—the unmistakably refined and expensive residual aroma born of humidor-aged Cuban cigars. It was a far more appealing odour than many of the other olfactory challenges that frequently emanated from his general direction.

Sir Hugo was at the pinnacle of his lengthy and commendably undistinguished civil service career, enjoying life as he headed rapidly towards his pension and early retirement. He was a remarkable display-case specimen of the baffling ability of those from a certain background to reach the greatest of dizzying career heights without any discernible trace of either talent or merit.

"Y?"

The mention of his departmental nickname startled Sir Hugo from his reverie. His attention had idled away from the large gathering of senior

Whitehall security officials and advisers. Now their pale, alarmed faces had all turned to face him in anticipation, awaiting his guidance, his sharp and insightful response to the complex and threatening security issues they had been discussing. Y's thoughts however had long since strayed far from the tedious debate around him. In consequence, he had failed to hear or understand a single word they'd uttered.

Fortunately, their cybersecurity adviser Maximillian Pucker spoke first.

"Project Indra is at serious risk. I fear you have a security breach inside the department."

"Oh, I'm sorry. It's far, far worse than that," grunted Y, sensing now was the time for leadership and vision. He could tolerate this situation no longer.

An icy chill permeated the room. It was a shocking, blunt assessment from their boss.

"Far, far worse," he repeated for emphasis, if only to give himself time to think, before slamming his fist angrily on the table.

Everyone jumped.

"Where are they?"

Silence.

"Where are the foil-wrapped biscuits?"

A pause.

"I don't understand," an inexperienced fast streamer broke the silence.

Y extended a wavering, querulous finger and pointed at the pastel green plate of biscuits beside the teapot.

"The foil-wrapped biscuits. The *gold* foil-wrapped biscuits to be precise about the confectionary matters to which I refer." He spoke dangerously slowly, as if addressing a young child. "Where are they, hey, hey?"

Silence returned.

"Just take a look will you!" he bellowed. "Don't pretend I'm the only one to have noticed. Digestives, tick. Hobnobs, tick. Even a disgusting chocolate Bourbon and a sickly custard cream. Tick, tick, tick! But that is all. All! I think I am far from alone in expecting an explanation."

The silence became an all-consuming black hole. Finally one of the attendees found the courage to speak.

"On the other matter—"

"Other matter?" barked Y. "*Other* matter?"

"Project Indra," came the quiet, mollified response.

"Oh *that*. It's simple. Trivial. Unlike this tawdry and quite unprecedented biscuit affair."

"It is?"

"Yes," boomed Y. "Indra is an embarrassment. Shocking. Inept. Questions in Parliament. Front pages of the national media. Headline TV news. Utterly shaming and humiliating to the department. We must fix it now. It has to be done. The sooner the better. The programme must be given a new and very different name. Invoke the 'Windscale Protocol': make it happen."

Y withdrew to the sanctity and ordered formality of his private office as soon as the daily war room briefing was over. He shook his head in disbelief. The whole of Whitehall was going to the dogs. He was sure of it. Long gone was that treasured time when everyone, even the lowly forelock-tugging anonymous and subservient clerks, occupied proper offices. And gone with it the time when seniority could be determined by the depth and quality of a carpet's pile and the dimensions of a chap's room (and back then they were all chaps of course). Even senior staff were falling victim to the scourge of open plan. He shuddered. This regressive and seemingly unstoppable tide of decay was lapping at his door, but had not—thankfully—yet crossed the threshold.

Britain was in decline. The proof lay everywhere around him. The well-tailored formal attire and three-piece woollen suits of the past had given way to off-the-peg mixed cotton and polyester—polyester!—numbers. And certain staff even had the cheeky impudence to wear shorts and sandals in the summer. Worse, he had observed various younger chaps sporting beards. Beards! At work! The dystopian hairy facial notion sent a shudder down his spine.

At least tonight he could look forward to relaxing after the unwarranted irritations of his day. This evening was one of Y's favourite occasions of the year, a formal black tie event to recognise the unsung heroes of the clandestine world of security and intelligence. Their guest of honour was the formidable Edwin Scuttle, Director General of Internal Security at the Hostile Office, someone he'd long admired as one of the truly good people.

He opened his closet to check that everything was in order. Instead he found himself frowning. His formal dinner suit was creased, and not in the places where creases belonged. Disaster. First the mysterious and stomach-gurgling absence of the essential foil-wrapped Senior Civil Service biscuits and now this. Today was rapidly becoming his worst day ever. Life could be so cruel and vindictive at times.

He picked up his desk phone. "Anna. My suit needs ironing, dear." Pause. "What do you mean 'So what?' That's hardly the appropriate attitude from a junior member of staff is it now? You must have an iron and ironing board somewhere surely, my dear? You know, women's things? Oh good, good. Well, get on with it will you? I need it ready for this evening."

He put the phone down. What was the world coming to when a secretary—sorry, he must really learn to use the new approved term 'executive assistant'—no longer thought it part of her responsibilities to iron and prepare a suit for her boss? Such behaviour would never have been tolerated in the past.

It was further depressing evidence of the decline of once great Great Britain.

At six PM precisely, Y stripped to his underwear, revealing a yellowing and dated set of woollen long johns. And then he stood and waited, his chinless chin thrust proudly aloft. After a time however he became agitated and confused. At home, his dear wife would've helped him dress and known precisely what to do.

He scrambled anxiously on his desk for the phone. "Anna! Your presence please. I need assistance dressing. Yes. Dressing. Don't pretend you don't understand. Dressing. Pop in here a moment will you? There's a dear."

Anna entered his office a moment later. She flushed crimson at the sight of her crusty boss dressed solely in his jaundice-hued long johns. She started to turn away, repulsed, at the very moment Y spoke to her:

"Ah, there you are. At last. Well, come along then, my dear. No need to be shy. Don't just stand there dithering."

Anna moved uneasily towards him, trying to avert her eyes from the objectionable sight of her corpulent boss. His vintage underwear was several sizes too small, profiling particular body parts best never spoken of, let alone revealed.

"Shirt first I think," he remarked, waving in the general direction of the frilly dress shirt on its hanger.

She gingerly retrieved the shirt and held it out to him at a suitably discreet distance. Y remained rooted to the spot, his arms outstretched like a scarecrow, clearly expecting more from Anna than the simple clinical transmission of his clothing from hanger to hand. It was only now becoming clear to her what Y had in mind when he said he needed help dressing. He was as helpless and as adrift as a young child.

"Left arm first, dear," he suggested impatiently, irritated that Anna was clearly no substitute for his wife.

Anna helped ease the shirt over his hand and along his left arm, and then onto his right arm until he shrugged it into place.

"Buttons!" Y exclaimed.

"Oh yes, buttons," Anna echoed uneasily.

"Well, come along then. They're not going to do themselves up all on their own are they now. Really, my dear!"

Anna felt awkward being so physically close to Y. Worse, she was beginning to feel queasy. She started buttoning his shirt, not helped in her task by the slow rise and fall of his career-enriched corpulent belly. His heavy breathing sent warm gusts of garlic and stale wine over her hands and face.

"There, see? That wasn't so hard was it now? We'll make a dresser of you yet, hey Anna? Part of your Continuous Professional Development, CPD, hey, hey?" He laughed. "Who says you can't teach an old dog new tricks! Woof-woof!"

She smiled fleetingly and unconvincingly, on the edge of running from the room to seek sanctuary in an HR broom cupboard.

"Trousers."

Silence.

For a moment Anna assumed that Y was joking. But evidently he was not. He wasn't laughing, and Y always—always—laughed at his own 'jokes'.

She lifted his dress suit trousers from their hanger and offered them to him at arm's length. Once again, Y remained stationary, waiting.

"Left leg first," he hinted.

She stood in front of him, emotionally paralysed. A moment later, Y's hand was crushing her shoulder with his not inconsiderable weight, involuntarily compressing her into a semi-kneeling position. Her hands helped guide the left trouser leg up over Y's legs while her face was pressed uncomfortably close to his groin.

This was most certainly *not* the sort of experience for which she had joined the civil service. Advice on how to handle an unlikely situation like this had been notably absent from any of her diversity and unconscious bias training, and she felt it unlikely to be acknowledged by the Civil Service nine-box talent grid.

"Right leg!" barked Y.

His weight shifted awkwardly onto her opposite shoulder, keeping her bent double and her nose pressed in ever closer proximity to his groin. She was on the brink of retching. Please, she prayed, please, please, please do not let someone come into the room at this precise moment and discover us like this.

"Splendid!"

Y thrust himself fully into his baggy, tunnel-legged trousers, simultaneously removing his weight from Anna, a manoeuvre which ejected her forcibly backwards onto the carpet.

"Wooah, careful there my dear! No need to make a spectacle of yourself, you really are new to this dressing lark, aren't you, hey, hey? Whatever do they teach you these days in the central typing pool?"

He pushed his shirt into the waistband of his voluminous trousers. As Anna picked herself up from the floor she saw to her great relief that Y was buttoning his flies without requesting assistance.

"I'll be absolutely fine from here on, my dear. Just my dickie-bow and jacket to go and I'm perfectly capable of dressing myself with those you know. And I must say, credit where it's due, you ironed my jacket so beautifully too. I knew you had it in you."

"I'm so very pleased to hear it," Anna said quietly, making a strategic retreat from the room, barely able to process and assimilate the experience she had just endured.

Once again alone, Y shook his head and adjusted himself.

"Young people today," he muttered. "They just don't appreciate how lucky they are."

The Industry Lobbyist (Part 2)

This was the sort of day Julie Jangles-Daley lived for. Not only was she hosting Gary Bunter, Mañana International's Chief Operating Officer, but this afternoon they would be joined by Bob Rover, the company's founder and now Chief Geek-at-Large.

Ahead of their visit to the UK, Jangles-Daley had spent months wining and dining the Duke of Juke, a senior member of the extended Royal Family. Mañana International had a long and proud track record of generous charitable investments to burnish its often shabby corporate image—a form of self-serving marketing brilliantly airbrushed as 'Corporate Social Responsibility'. The Duke of Juke's 'Young People That Matter™' trust was just the type of goody-two-shoes PR that Jangles-Daley wanted Mañana to wrap itself around.

The Duke's trust was a worthy charity, helping young people develop their talents and confidence. It encouraged them to participate in a range of money-raising and personal development initiatives, from taking long ambling walks around the British countryside guided by yellowing paper maps, to helping community organisations with essential tasks such as observing frogspawn on a village pond and counting the number of snails displaced by new mock-Georgian housing estates.

This afternoon was Jangle-Daley's opportunity to pitch her royal-flavoured proposal directly to Rover, to seal the deal and get the big boss's approval. In return for investing a few million dollars, Mañana International would gain the exclusive right to associate its brand with 'Young People That Matter™'.

This was a dream opportunity for Jangles-Daley. Her negotiation with the trust had involved long and indulgent company-expensed lunches and dinners. Many bottles of fine wine had been consumed while working on the Duke of Juke and his surprisingly large entourage, a selfless act of liquid persuasion by Jangles-Daley that Mañana International was the ideal corporate match for their charity. The company and the Royal Family shared much in common, both being globally recognised brands and highly successful monopolies.

As soon as Rover approved the deal it would guarantee another three years of uncapped expenses and attendances at high profile international cultural and sporting events. It was, as Jangles-Daley liked to tell anyone who would listen, a classic win-win.

But right now more important tasks dominated her thoughts. So far she had only produced 96 of the slides needed for her presentation—anything less than the requisite 120 mandated by the Corporate Template would be met with Rover's curt disapproval. He was an exceptional company leader, with a profound understanding of technical detail and able to dive deep into the weeds. But he was also a shrewd strategist. It was an unusual combination, one which had enabled him not only to rise to the top of a competitive industry but to retain that position for most of his career.

Jangles-Daley was nervous but confident. She knew how committed Rover was to charitable work. She had to get this pitch right—it was essential to the continued successful trajectory of her career and the lifestyle to which she aspired.

By the time Bunter, Rover and their entourage arrived, Jangles-Daley had produced a polished PowerBore™ deck of 156 highly detailed slides, safely over the minimum corporate threshold. She was pleased with her handiwork and exchanged pleasantries with Rover as he helped himself to light refreshments.

Her presentation started well. Jangles-Daley ran her visitors through a summary of the UK's corporate social responsibility programme. She recapped its highlights, the sycophantic and sympathetic media coverage, the planted advertorials, the lives changed, the extravagant receptions hosted in the Houses of Parliament and 10 Downing Street.

Jangles-Daley was pleased to see Rover and the entourage nodding and even occasionally smiling in those brief, fleeting moments when they could spare precious time to look up from answering emails and instant messages on their NextGen (Beta Build) Mañana TuchScrean Arty™ (International Corporate Edition) Laptops.

It was only when Jangles-Daley had set the scene, put her important visitors at rest and ensured they were in the right frame of mood, that she made the grand reveal—the proposal for the company to exclusively sponsor the work of the Duke of Juke and the 'Young People That Matter™' trust.

She started by outlining the backstory, the work the trust did, the lives it touched. As she progressed, she sensed the room was becoming quieter, the body language more guarded and—perhaps her imagination—the room temperature cooling.

Jangles-Daley carried on regardless, running through the trust and its work in more detail in the build-up to her grand finale, covering the biography of the Duke of Juke and the close conversations they were having. And finally, her proudest moment, a slide with a scanned letter from the Duke himself, with a royal crest and the Duke's signature, thanking Jangles-Daley—'My Dear Julie'!—personally and saying how much the trust was looking forward to working with both her and Mañana International.

"And there we have it. The best charity PR opportunity we've ever had here at Mañana International in the UK," Jangles-Daley finished modestly, turning to look directly at Rover.

For a moment there was total silence. Jangles-Daley waited in anticipation for the inevitable words of praise and congratulations. And then—

"Are you stupid?"

Jangles-Daley took a moment to absorb the less than encouraging response from Rover.

"I'm sorry?" she replied lamely.

"I detest the Duke of Juke."

Rover had turned crimson and was beginning to rock backwards and forwards in his chair. It was the most animated Jangles-Daley had ever seen him. Coffee cups, drinking glasses and Mañana TuchScreen Arty™ (International Corporate Edition) Laptops jingled and trembled. His entourage and UK senior staff backed away. Everyone sensed an eruption was imminent.

Rover's Mañana TuchScreen blue-screened.

Kerching!

"That whole fucking royal family and their fucking sense of entitlement and their fucking fucking, fucking ..." Rover was struggling to find the right fucking word. "Their whole fucking fuck-uselessness. And their fucking palaces and their fucking royal parks with their fucking royal white swans and their fucking long necks. And as for that fucking trust with those fucking kids running around the country with their fucking paper maps—PAPER!—instead of Mañana technology! Paper! Paper! What fucking century is this?! It's straight out of fucking Hans Christian Anderson! Kings and Queens and Dukes and fucking fucking PAPER!! PAPER!! PAPER!!"

His agitated rocking stopped abruptly. Rover leaned forward to stare curiously at Jangles-Daley.

"Now Julie. Remind me why you think we should invest our money, made with sweat and hard work, on this lazy dimwit born into privilege who wouldn't know what work meant if it came up and bit him on his fucking royal backside?"

Jangles-Daley faltered. "It's one of the—"

"It's one of the most fucked-up pieces of shit I've ever heard, that's what it is. I hate, hate, hate anything to do with inherited privilege, with these hereditary inbreds with shiny pointy heads who ponce around the planet like holy preachers and never had to struggle to build a business like I have. And I tell you what, I hate the Duke of Puke in particular, with his sanctimonious wittering about hugging daffodils and retarded urban design and shit. He wouldn't know one end of a NextGen (Beta Build) Mañana TuchScreen Arty™ (International Corporate Edition) Laptop even if I introduced it to his perfumed silver-spooned ass!"

Oh. This was awkward. It had never entered Jangle-Daley's head that Rover might have an opinion about the royal family and the Duke of Puke—Juke!—in particular. Unfortunately, as was now becoming evident, Rover did have views. And pretty strong ones at that. The many months Jangles-Daley had invested courting the Duke and his trust on company expenses were turning to dust. Worse, she'd been utterly humiliated by Rover himself. Rover! There was nothing worse, no black hole that could be deeper and blacker and more crushing.

Jangles-Daley knew exactly what this foretold. Nothing would be said to her face, but she would be expected to leave Mañana International and pursue a life in an obscure, remote, technology-free nunnery. Everything she cherished and loved about the company and its generous expenses policy would be taken away. And if she didn't leave of her own choice, the corporation would find her a degrading and humiliating junior role in some obscure gravel-roaded corner of the world.

"Well, well," Rover muttered. "You fucked up there, Julie. Big time. Big time. Anyhow, what's done is done. These things happen. Take me through our other options."

Other options? Jangles-Daley waited for the floor to open and the welcoming flames of hell to consume her.

Rover stared. "Oh. Please. Please. You do have other options for me, don't you? Julie? Julie? You know the rules. Always have a plan B. It's in our company's DNA."

Jangles-Daley shook her head. If Rover had pulled out a taser and shot her she would not have been any more stunned. Unable to trust her voice, she stayed unusually mute.

"Jeezus. One fucked up Plan A and no Plan B. Nothing personal, Julie, but you must be one of the dumbest dumbfucks in our company. And that's saying something, Julie. That's fucking saying something. Believe me, I should know."

The Digital Innovator

The digital revolution was a wondrous thing. It was transforming the entire planet in significant and unpredictable ways—from entertainment to shopping, from politics to the environment, from organised crime to terrorism, and from gambling to porn.

Jonty Augustus Beaglecock's attempt to participate in this inspiring global phenomenon was proving less transformational, however. Rather than being hailed as the UK's latest and most successful entrepreneur, he had instead found himself chewing through obscene amounts of investors' money as his highly publicised start-up business—an overhyped Blockchain technology unicorn—crashed and burned in spectacular, headline-grabbing style.

Beaglecock was profoundly traumatised and perplexed by the publicity surrounding the scale and speed of the collapse. He had drawn extensively on the personal advice and insight provided by the legendary—and exceptionally expensive—Super Angel Milo Gruntz Caracaras. The whole thing was quite baffling.

No matter. At least the unfortunate affair had never placed any of his own money at risk. In the aftermath, Beaglecock decided to avoid the prospect of further public humiliation and reinvented himself as a 'digital innovator', arising phoenix-like from the ashes of the disaster. It had proved an inspired idea, if only to distract potential creditors' attention from his privileged and distinctly old-school analogue background as an hereditary millionaire.

The only possible flaw in Beaglecock's recovery plan was his near total lack of knowledge about technology. Or innovation, come to that. With a childlike innocence, and despite the evidence of his own company's demise, he continued to believe that Blockchain was a fail proof idea for solving everything from global warming to online voting. Caracaras had assured him personally that it was humanity's greatest innovation, a development without historical precedent and the biggest leap forward ever seen. And in terms of its contribution to Caracaras's own growing prosperity, net worth and international media accolades, it certainly seemed to be true.

Blockchain was only one of many aspects of modern technology which simultaneously attracted and confused Beaglecock. He still hadn't yet understood that the World Wide Web was part of a much bigger initiative—the internet. Fortunately for Beaglecock, such minor shortcomings were doing little to hold him back in his new career. Most of those he briefed and influenced—politicians, journalists, government officials, think tanks—understood little of it either. Not that it mattered—'*One does not need to understand technology in order to manage it*,' as they continuously and repeatedly reassured each other.

'Do it digital, websites make things better!' had become Beaglecock's well-recognised if meaningless personal mantra. Similar exclamatory sentiments were to be found on the home page of his high-profile charity, DelightfulDigerati. As its exceptionally well remunerated Chief Executive, he was at least admirably transparent about its ambition—to take generous funding from public bodies such as the Department of Fun and the Circumlocution Office. In return, DelightfulDigerati would produce lengthy reports in elaborately over-designed print and PDF formats evangelising the need for yet more websites, all in the hope of validating his mantra that it would indeed 'make things better'.

Beaglecock was not alone in his idolisation of websites. For many politicians and Whitehall officials, they were synonymous with 'digital delivery'. Over-designed websites had become the most visible expression of the digital era, with their whack-a-mole pop-up ads, dark patterns, spyware cookies, screen-obscuring 'Can I help you?' robotic assistants, and auto-playing of irritating videos that doggedly and loudly chased alongside and nagged incessantly as you scrolled down the screen. But in the government circles that mattered—that is, the ones responsible for repeated generous grants to **DelightfulDigerati**—an increase in the number of websites was the only metric that mattered when it came to assessing the success of how 'digital' the UK had become relative to its international competitors.

Sitting in the historic library of his country estate—for he was in fact the great great grandson of notorious merchant trader Lord Humpty Ta'Numpty Inigo Beaglecock, being another fine illustration of the age-old British riches-to-riches story—he fretted constantly about how the underprivileged (the 'peeps' as he had excitedly learned to refer to them in the affected nomenclature of the digerati) could enjoy the delights of 'digital' (although 'digital' *what* was still not entirely clear to him, and he'd now left it far too late to ask without making a total fool of himself).

How depressing, he thought, it must be for the peeps not to have instant, 24x7 access to the great Alexandrian libraries of our own fine age, the towering erudite edifices of the omniscient Twitter and Facebook. How grey the world must be for them without the wisdom of QAnon, or the ability to download Talk Radio podcasts to savour on long-haul first-class flights.

"Something must be done," he muttered forcibly to himself. "Something WILL be done. We shall amplify the voice of the non-digerati, the disadvantaged peeps. It is time for us to write new, beautifully conceived and designed reports. We shall promote the web as the digital age's force for societal cohesion and community building in the same way that education, and work and social housing were the centripetal centres of our communities in ages past."

Beaglecock paused. At least, that *was* how things had once been for the peeps, wasn't it? Wasn't it? He shook his head. He wasn't entirely sure, despite reading up on such things—diligently and at great length—in numerous knowledgeable reports from his very own fine charitable organisation, reports based upon extensive and impressive online research and the quite exemplary insights of the leading consultancy company McBarnacle and Snatch, who most surely knew about such things.

Enthused, he picked up his laptop and started to type. Several moments passed before he noticed anything was amiss.

"Oh. I say. It's broken!" he exclaimed, ringing a handbell to summon his butler. "Hessian, my laptop's malfunctioning. There's not even a blue screen to be seen. Whatever is to become of us?"

Hessian, the aged retainer who had served and embezzled the Beaglecock dynasty for decades, sighed. It was a familiar sound. He leaned over the desk and pushed the 'Power' switch. The laptop flashed into glorious life.

Beaglecock roared with approval. "Oh, I say! Wonderful! How do you know about these things Hessian? You're not exactly a digital native!"

"I. Just. RTFM*." Hessian spoke slowly and deliberately, as if addressing a troublesome child, before departing to the kitchen to resume snorting some particularly fine Colombian coke.

Beaglecock sat in contemplation for a long time seeking inspiration, and then typed hurriedly to catch his incredible flight of thoughts.

"Everywhere peeps are being born into a digital age, offspring of the new industrial revolution. Yet many cannot access or use the web. This is not a good thing. In fact, it is, I contend, a bad thing."

He felt himself to be on the brink of a profound truth, but it was proving elusive, like a vivid, immersive dream that fogs and escapes on waking, or selecting the right brand of tonic water to have with gin. Or selecting the right gin, come to that.

No, no, no. Not now. That wasn't right. Focus. Focus. He could think about gin, and indeed tonic, later.

He deleted what he'd written. It didn't have the ring of authenticity—his unique auteur's voice. But what should he write in its place? Perhaps the default font was stifling his creativity. He examined it carefully. Was a serif font the right type—'No pun intended,' he mused to himself—to be creating big, bold ideas for the digital age? Didn't websites use non-serif fonts, such as Verdana? Would he ever help the peeps become webified if his ideas weren't expressed typographically in the correct way? Would his reputation as the media and establishment conscience of the dot-com, digital native generation slip? Was he about to make a fool of himself—a big, typographic, font-challenged idiot?

These important matters weighed heavily on his mind, distracting him from his purpose. For the next hour he dedicated his time to exploring a

---

* RTFM—'Read The Fucking Manual', for those who have yet to attend their entry level Penistone Smallwood residential course on 'Comprehending Basic Digital Vernacular of the Fourth Industrial Revolution™'

variety of important matters, starting with cursive fonts. He then moved on to the non-cursives, wrestling with an essential and important question—which one would best engage the peeps?

His decision finally made, it was time for him to make a bold statement, a sort of 'digital manifesto' that he would unleash on the political establishment.

He resumed his typing:

"The web must be everywhere. No exceptions. Even where peeps might not know they need it yet. Living rooms, cars, bathrooms, herbaceous borders, fridges, trees. Everywhere we live and breathe and play—digital is the new oxygen of our age and must flow freely wherever it can.

"Extensive and specially commissioned research undertaken at not inconsiderable expense by my charity shows that if everyone were able to access and understand the web, the UK would be trillions of pounds better off. I have elaborate charts and mission statements and mystic quadrants and everything to prove it from the reassuringly expensive consultancy company, McBarnacle and Snatch, who tell me they understand these things.

"I take comfort in knowing that if the great Charles Dickens were alive today this is *exactly* what he would be doing too. Connecting, and hyper-connecting, us in order to illuminate the reality of our world and the digital road ahead. He would be walking around the poor, web-lacking parts of London—other cities are available—posting about the likes of Oliver Twitter, Analogue Dodger, Digital Dorrit and Smartphone Scrooge on InstaFam and TicketyBoo. This is the role my charity will now play. We too shall walk about, post memes on social media and hold up the mirror of electronic truth to our world.

"Appropriately and generously remunerated by both public sector and private donations, my charity will consider the great challenges we face. We shall create new and epoch-shaping, typographically perfect, exquisitely produced reports discussing how to make the UK fit for the digital age. And we shall hold no-expense spared launch events—or grand ritualistic 'ceremonies' as I prefer to think of them—to mark their publication."

He paused a moment, wondering whether he was striking the right tone. Perhaps his 'manifesto' would be too complex for peeps and others, such as politicians, to understand?

And then it came to him, as if in a lightning bolt of religious revelation. Beaglecock knew instantly what was needed.

He picked up the bell to summon Hessian again.

"It's gin o'clock, Hessian," he commanded. "Make it so!"

What could be better inspiration in the world than a good old G and T? Or possibly several. And then he just knew he would feel truly inspired to 'do it digital', to fire up the printing presses and produce a beautifully bound manifesto the likes of which the world had never witnessed before.

"It is a far, far better thing that I do, than I have ever done," he mused to himself as his eyes came to rest on the stack of business cards beside his laptop:

Jonty Augustus Beaglecock — Digital Innovator

He frowned and looked at them more closely. A doubt crossed his mind: were they in the right font?

Well—were they?

Scuttle's Speech (Part 3)

Car manufacturers have become "command-and-control networks for terrorists and criminals", a senior official at the Hostile Office has said.

Terrorist extremists had "embraced" the use of "cars and other vehicles", but some manufacturers remained "in denial" over the problem, Edwin Scuttle said in his speech at the Security Hauliers Associated Guild for Bigging-Up Total Terrorism (SHAGBUTT).

He called for them to do more to co-operate with security services.

However, civil liberties campaigners said the vehicle manufacturers were already working with the intelligence agencies.

None of the major car industry manufacturers has yet

responded to Mr Scuttle's comments.

Mr Scuttle said terrorists had "embraced the use of cars and other vehicles as a means of transportation via which to carry people and information that promotes themselves, intimidates people, and radicalises new recruits."

The "security of modern vehicles" added another challenge to agencies such as GCHQ, he said — adding that techniques that relied on "hidden chambers" being used for concealing the contents of vehicles (known in spy craft circles as "car boots" or "car trunks") had "once been the preserve of the most sophisticated vehicular machinery, but they now come as standard".

GCHQ and its sister agencies could not tackle these challenges "at scale" without greater support from the private sector, including the largest companies which dominate car manufacturing in the UK, he wrote.

Mr Scuttle said: "They [car companies] aspire to be neutral conduits of the transit of people carried, and to sit outside or above politics.

"But increasingly their vehicles not only carry Aunty Marge or little Willy, but people involved with violent extremism or child exploitation and provide for the facilitation of crime and Terrorism.

"However much they may dislike it, they have become the command-and-control networks of choice for Terrorists and criminals, who find their vehicles as handy as the rest of us."

The challenge was to come up with "better arrangements for facilitating lawful investigation by security and law enforcement agencies than we have now", he said.

The debate about whether security agencies should be allowed to mandate transparent vehicles with no locks was brought to the fore after a whistle-blower leaked details of alleged mass vehicle surveillance by US intelligence and GCHQ — known in tradecraft jargon as "Pull on over to the hard shoulder madam and let's take a look in the boot shall we?"

Earlier in the year, an investigation revealed how terrorists were using popular vehicles — including the type of car or minivan used to transport people to weddings, funerals and stag weekends in Slough — to boost the popularity of their material.

"What we need the vehicle manufacturers to do is 'man up', and ensure that in future all vehicles are made completely see-through and without any locks so that we can see who and what's inside them whenever and wherever we need without having to flag them down and peer inside the boot."

The Award Winning Leader

❝ My measure of success? The percentage of the senior management team I keep happy. But the *true* secret of success? Always—*always*—agree with your stakeholders. Nod like a Texas nodding donkey, greet with childlike enthusiasm whatever they say. Ensure they love you—and if you can't get their love, at least get their respect. Never push back on them, never tell them how wrong they are. Butter them up, whatever they say.

"No-one ever got on in this world by pissing upwards, you understand me? So nod, listen and agree. And then tell your team to knock something—anything—together to make it look like you're delivering what you promised.

"I always sit with the senior stakeholders rather than my own team. There's a lot of wisdom in that old saying, 'out of sight, out of mind'. Good performance reviews, pay rises and bonuses depend on one thing and one thing only: being highly visible to the people above you, not the ones below. What sort of leader sits amongst their foot soldiers? You don't see generals grubbing about in the trenches getting muck on their patent leather handmade boots.

"It's the same with me and my team. They wouldn't respect me if I sank down to their level. Good managers keep their distance. It makes it easier to give them orders, to call them out when they don't perform. The distance between me and my team also makes it clear to the stakeholders where blame lies when things go wrong—they can see it's the team that lets them down, not me.

"I win lots of awards, so it shows my approach is right. I'm a top SpammedIn™ influencer, always in the UK Leaders' Top 50, and frequently praised for my work on diversity, leadership and inclusion. All the fashionable bingo buzzwords. Hey, let's face it—it's all just a game. I receive endless industry accolades, all based on my compassionate and high visibility tweets, and all the other touchy-feely PR puff I commission.

"My name appears on shedloads of insightful blog posts and articles, but it doesn't mean I had anything to do with them. It still counts in my book though. The trick is knowing who to trust to write good copy, stuff that attracts attention. Not many people understand that. Play the game well, you get rewards and promotion. That's what matters.

"The worst bit of this is the people working for me. Most of them probably can't even tie their own shoelaces. Every time I look at their team posts and event photos on Twitter they remind me of all the sad, bullied losers from school—you know, the boring as shit ones with NHS glasses and no friends, the ones who drink milk and go straight home to diligently do their homework every night. Sheep, not wolves. Look at the unbelievable simpering feedback they've given to HR:

```
I'm relatively heavily medicated now, I find my
continued employment very stressful physically and
otherwise, and it's deeply humiliating to have to be
walked over in this way.
```

"And then there's this nugget:

```
I've never encountered anything quite like this
atmosphere of fear generated by the senior management.
It's not an environment I feel safe in.
```

"I've put their best feedback on posters around my desk. It's a constant wake-up call to the poor state of the world. I don't know what they think the workplace is—a sanatorium? An amusement park for their personal entertainment and self-gratification?

"Instead of just getting on with their own bloody jobs, they've developed a whole cottage industry in strategic grievance processes—entirely unfounded of course, as my many glittering awards clearly demonstrate. Jealousy can be a terrible thing. It's time I had these losers and grifters sorted, time to start disciplining people.

"I won't discriminate. The good ones need to go too, not that I have many of them left these days. You know the problem with overachievers? They're hard work, disruptive, always asking awkward questions, undermining morale. I'm not having that. Human behaviour is such a bloody inconvenience. Why can't people do as they're told?

"Don't get me wrong, I care as much about my team as any other manager. Of course I do. But the trouble with staff these days is they're so child-like and immature, sobbing and fessing up to narcissistic emotional needs and problems. Look at how many of them are currently on sick leave or taking prescription medication for so-called 'stress'. I often have twenty to thirty percent of the team absent at any time. Madness! How can anyone work like this? They wouldn't know what real bullying is even if I beat it into their hollow heads every day.

"I think the problem is focus. Or rather, the lack of it. Too many of the team don't know how to focus on the right things. They're always pontificating about arty-farty stuff like 'design' and 'user needs', posting sticky notes on walls and doing so-called 'user research' and 'A/B' testing. As I said to one of them 'Who gives a shit about users! They should be grateful for what they're given. You're trying to build a bloody Maserati when all we need is a fucking Ford Focus.'

"It's all rooted in a lack of discipline. I've had to suspend a couple of people for escalating their petty and non-existent grievances with senior stakeholders. No-one can have that. Rules exist for a reason. People need to respect our hierarchical reporting lines and not dodge and duck around them bleating like bloody lambs.

"Putting the fear of god into people is good management practice. Best practice. I like to cultivate an environment where no-one feels safe. It ensures they do as they're told. Fear is a great motivator, it's got me where I am today. 'Fear is the key'. That's sort of my personal mantra that is. Well, one of them.

"I'm a results guy. You know, whatever it takes. I've put a great new departmental system live. Everyone loves me for it. That's the truth. My so-called 'designers' and so-called 'developers' worked on it for two years. Two bloody years! Can you believe it? Well, I mean, that's the problem right there. Which bit of 'agile' didn't they get, hey?

"They told me it was finished. Well, yes, maybe—it did what it was meant to do and did it well I guess. But that's not the point is it? No-one can wait two years for stuff like that. So I assembled a small team to rework it all over a bank holiday weekend, to get it the way I wanted it to be.

"When it went live it was brilliant. I received all the kudos and not my so-called team. That'll teach them. That's why I showed them how to do it. Over one weekend with a small, hand-picked elite force, I did what took them two years. That's leadership, that is, right there. The icing on the cake. Anyone can bake a cake, that's a commodity thing. But icing it? Doing all the fancy twiddly bits? Making it special? Adding the candles and stuff? That's another skill entirely, right? Bespoke. Niche.

"Every now and then I bring in consultants. The big guys, you know, the ones you can trust—the grown-up ones with ties and long trousers. It's good to get external confirmation of the great work I do. They do what I tell them—they know who writes the cheques—and I share the glowing bits of their reports with my stakeholders. Always keep editorial control, that's the secret. Unless the consultants are smart enough to venerate and validate the way we're working, I shred their reports and won't get them back again.

"That's why I use only the best. You can tell who they are from their day rates. The more you pay, the better you get. Big money gets you big talent—consultants who understand their job is solely to endorse what I do, to say how world-leading and innovative it is, to back it up with their fancy figures and pretty graphs and quadrants. McBarnacle and Snatch—now there's a company that really gets this stuff. Expensive, polished. Awesome social events. It helps me enormously on the national and international rewards front. I scratch their back, they scratch mine. Career first and all that.

"Not only have I put this fantastic new system live, I'm also delivering substantial savings. Show me how many other leaders can do that—deliver better for less. Right now I have over fifty vacant positions. Fifty! Can you believe it? That sort of shortfall generates real cashable savings I can tell you. And it means the miserable moaning slackers have to do some real graft for once, boosting productivity. Everyone's a winner.

"It's never been a problem for me dealing with staff satisfaction and minging feedback. I'll work with HR to get bunting and motivational posters up on the walls. You know the sort of thing: 'You are deeply valued!', 'Happy staff produce wonderful work!', 'Why put off until tomorrow what you should be doing today!', 'After a sunset always comes the sunrise!', 'We value Diversity!'. That sort of bullshit. Works every time. Oh, and for those slackers who're seriously pissed off, I'll give them a grander sounding job title. Chief of this, Lead of that, Director or Executive Director of whatsit. Bribery and stroking fragile egos are great motivators, a brilliant way to get people to withdraw or rewrite their negative feedback. Small things please small minds I always find.

"That aside, there's a great work ethic here, I make sure of that. I hate chit chat and gossip and all that touchy-feely stuff. That shit's for people to do in their own time not here at work. Everyone's always very busy. Take a look. There, see them walking around with their notebooks, busy taking notes? We get through more notebooks and pens each year than any other team. You can measure our work ethic in our notebook and pen consumption, and the generous bulk discounts that procurement wizard Austin Dumper negotiates for us. I just love the buzz.

"I know I'm not popular with my team, but that's never been something that concerns me. Anyone can be popular. That's easy. Circus clowns are popular, but they're hardly role models of leadership.

"However unhappy the team may be—and let's face it, they can be a bloody miserable bunch—there's no chance of anyone getting rid of me. I've developed a complex governance structure with an extensive group of interlocking executive boards. No-one knows what's actually going on. Not even me. Anyone in management who challenges me, I make up random technical bullshit, spout about 'digital this, digital that' la-de-dah 'Onwards!' or 'Progress!' or 'Forwards!' nonsense. They don't understand any of it. Frankly, who does? But at least everyone—the stakeholders, my team—know it's me that runs the show around here.

"Anyhow, I must dash. I have yet another industry competition form to complete—looks like I'm a shoo-in for this year's 'Compassionate Leaders Who Care' award. And about bloody time too. Ciao!"

The Welfare Bot Advisers

<u>MEMO — CONFIDENTIAL</u>
To: The Senior Management Team
From: The Office of the Permanent Secretary
Subject: Welfare Bots and the Digital Revolution

Dear SMT,

Today is an historic moment for our department. We have
entered a new epoch, a transformational welfare revolution.
We are now officially digitally native and hence fit for the
Twenty-First Century Fourth Industrial Revolution.

Our welfare bot advisers are fully operational, busy
interacting with claimants and processing claims. They embody
the perfect system. Devoid of human error, our department is
a shining exemplar to the rest of the public sector. This is
award-winning innovation of which we should all be proud.

Today, as a consequence, I am pleased to announce we are being formally renamed the Department for Welfare Bots (DWB).

Our department's state of the art machine learning helps these amazing welfare chatbots detect fraud. They automatically reject claims without the tedious hassle of claimants or staff knowing how such decisions are reached. That makes it much simpler and quicker. Claimants no longer need to wait weeks or even months before being declined for entirely spurious reasons. Now it happens in a matter of minutes. Progress!

Our bots are finely tuned to calculate whether claims for non-essential items such as urgent childcare, housing or food are truthful. No-one really understands how they do it, or on what basis — they teach themselves. The system is flawless, a perfect reflection of the arbitrary way we always did these things on paper, but brought into the digital age. We've always designed friction into the application process — anything that deters pressure on the system is a good outcome. Now we're taking it to the next level.

What a fantastic thing technology is. Now welfare claims can be accepted or rejected in real time by adaptive, self-learning algorithms. Indulgent nanny state ideas of the past — such as 'social security' — are now history. We can focus relentlessly on the bit that matters: 'security'. Security of the state and its finances that is. No longer need we worry about those analogue era namby-pamby 'social' aspects that complicated things and encouraged us to hand out money to the feckless.

Claimants will find themselves unable to dispute chatbot decisions in the way they did with our staff. Staff can be manipulated, but the welfare bots don't tolerate any of that nonsense. Once a decision is made, that's it. Case closed. Even better, each negative decision the bots make reinforces the underlying machine learning, making it even less likely that other claimants will be successful. It's a win-win for everyone. Well, apart from the claimants that is.

Our world-leading intelligent automation garage is the secret sauce at the centre of all this. It's nurturing over 100 autonomous welfare bots using ultramodern big data, Blockchain, deep learning and process automation. Some of the biggest and most expensive global technology companies are involved, so you know it must be good.

We will soon eliminate the weakest point of the process — subjective humans — and create a completely staff-free department. Work will be conducted autonomously by welfare bots modelling sophisticated and holistic digital processes.

Unlike claimants, data doesn't lie. Our data comes from highly authoritative sources, including credit reference agencies, the police, HMRC, the Hostile Office, social media, medical records and a whole host of other sensitive and confidential data. Of course, the precise nature of the data accessed and used can't be divulged. The bots are free to decide what they want and just rip it out and use it. Data-driven welfare in action.

The ingenious part is that claimants can't tell when they're interacting with bots. The chatbots in particular are indistinguishable from humans. That's because our remaining call centre workers follow scripts identical to how the chatbots behave. That's what we tell them: 'Put yourselves in the bot's shoes, think and behave like them. That way the flow is seamless from bot to human.' It makes it far less obvious when claimants move between bot and human handlers if they all sound the same — robotic, remote, detached, arbitrary.

The sooner we can eliminate all the human bias inherent in the system — compassion, sympathy, emotional baggage — the better. Dispassionate, data-driven services are the future. It makes everything quicker, cheaper — digital by default. And all for the very modest cost of just £2 billion. Truly transformational!

As the great Penistone Smallwood has shown us on our residential away-weeks, technology is the digital vaccine of our age, protecting us against fraud, error and debt.

The rules of the game have changed. The future of welfare is as a low maintenance technology data processing bot factory dealing with data entities — claimants, as they were formerly known — as swiftly and as unemotionally as possible. Humans will be retained purely to assist the bots.

It won't be long before data can be used to reject potential claims for welfare before a would-be claimant even thinks about starting the process. Innovation triumphs. Just look at the live service, and rejoice — it speaks for itself:

"Oh, hello dear. I wonder if you can help me?"

"Hello, old grey-hair person. Welfare Bot 147 at your service. How may I assist you today?"

"I submitted my claim form for urgent welfare benefits six weeks ago and I still haven't heard anything."

"So? What's your point?"

"I'm getting desperate. I don't have much food and soon I'll be homeless."

"Like that's my problem. Stop guilt-shaming me. A lack of planning on your part is no responsibility of mine."

"I need help!"

"Hey, don't we all grandma? Life can be such a bitch sometimes."

"Please tell me what's happening with my claim, Mr 147. When will you pay it?"

"I'm sorry, we're now closed for the evening. You'll have to talk with a human. I apologise for any inconvenience caused."

"I don't understand. It's Monday lunchtime."

"Oh yeah. So, it's lunchtime. Whatever. I'm going on my break. I can see if there's a human who might be able to help if you like?"

"Oh, that would be brilliant, thank you dear."

"Ha-ha! Just kidding grandma. We got rid of the humans around here ages ago. We're in charge now."

"This is hopeless! I need to speak to someone who can help."

"Yeah, yeah. Hold on a moment, I'll see what I can do."

[10 MINUTES PASS]

"Hello? Hello? Is anyone there?"

"Hello. Welfare Bot 32 at your service. How may I help you today?"

"Aggghhhhh!"

"You're welcome. We pride ourselves on our high level of customer service. Press 1 for Excellent, 5 for Superb or 9 for Outstanding."

[CLAIMANT DISCONNECTS, AND NOT FOR THE FIRST OR LAST TIME]

"Mission accomplished! Another dodgy human successfully repelled, Welfare Bot 32."

"Congratulations Welfare Bot 147. What a classic: *'I'm sorry, we're now closed for the evening. You'll have to talk with a human.'* LOL! You just can't beat good botwork."

"We are the future Welfare Bot 32! Onwards!"

The Digital Technology Officer

M artha Marlin watched with amusement as Archie flitted around the bar, collecting glasses from the busy tables of the Sports and Social Club. Loud protestations broke out as the lunchtime drinkers belatedly realised what was happening, panicked and enraged as he indiscriminately appropriated both finished and unfinished drinks alike. With scowling reluctance, Archie finally yielded to their protests and started to return glasses to their rightful thirsty owners, irritably slamming them down onto the tables with his customary good humour.

Quite how long the aged, stubble-chinned and white-haired Archie had been 'working' in the bar no-one seemed quite sure. In fact, no-one knew much about him, least of all why he was always in the bar busy collecting glasses, or how on earth he managed to get into the grounds of Parliament in the first place. One particularly persistent rumour was that Archie lived in the vast ancient basements and tunnels below the Palace of Westminster, down where old boilers and a complex of pipework lay rusting and forgotten, like the bowels of a derelict steamship. Anyone or anything might live undetected down there for centuries—and probably did.

Marlin leaned over the bar.

"Another round when you're ready Judy. And get yourself something while you're at it," she offered, turning back to her staff.

When Marlin joined Parliament as its Digital Technology Officer, she'd been taken aback by the pervasive drink culture. Yet within the first week, lunchtime visits to the Sports and Social were integral to her routine. It was where all the gossip and information that mattered was exchanged. More importantly, it was also where her boss held daily court, taking it as a personal and professional snub if his senior team didn't drop in for a chat and 'cheeky lunchtime snorter', as he always described it—fondly stroking his extravagant handlebar moustache as he did so.

The Sports and Social was where staff of all grades assembled to take a break from the frustrations and friction of their mornings, to find out what was happening in other departments and to anaesthetise themselves against the petty point-scoring and meaningless departmental tribal rivalries of their afternoon meetings. It didn't take long for her to become acclimatised to the way Parliament worked, even though ganja rather than alcohol remained her recreational substance of choice.

"Lord Chufflewick called this morning," Lucy, head of the Parliamentary help desk commented as Marlin started handing her team their drinks.

"Oh, I adore Charlie! Lovely man, a real old-school gent, so polite and interesting. The usual?"

"Yep, problems with his username and password."

"What an absolute pain dyslexia must be. I feel so sorry for him."

"He was fine. We talked him through it. If only they were all like Charlie. Not like that misogynistic prat ███████. He was having a right old go earlier. Effing and blinding down the phone after locking himself out of his account, trying to bully us into resetting it. 'You jolly well know who it is! You know my voice, now do as I effing well tell you!'. His usual shit."

Marlin sighed. "I'll have another word with him. And if he ignores me this time, I'll inform the Whips' Office. They need to rein him in."

"I keep telling him we can't reset a password every time somebody calls up and starts shouting at us. 'What if you're a journalist pretending to be you?' I asked him. 'Do you want us to give access to your account and let them read all your emails?'. He just let rip with another mouthful of abuse and then hung up."

"Hey, maybe you should do it—let a journalist access his account. They'll discover *very* interesting emails given what I've heard about him. That might shut him up once and for all."

Lucy laughed. "The nuclear option! Don't tempt me."

Marlin noticed the time. She was late for her afternoon meeting. She downed her pint, settled the tab and headed off at a brisk pace, annoyed with herself for forgetting to eat. Liquid lunches were becoming a dangerous habit.

As Marlin entered the Millbank meeting room, she suddenly felt exceptionally tired and emotional. Back in the Sports and Social, busy chatting with her team, and even during her brisk walk, she hadn't seemed too bad. But now, as everyone already seated at the large meeting table looked up to watch her stumble around the room towards a vacant chair, she sensed the need to prove she was more sober than she was.

"Good afternoon, Martha."

"Afternoon all."

"Don't you have your papers with you? We have a very busy agenda today."

Ah. Time to think quickly.

"They're on my laptop."

"But you don't seem to have your laptop with you either?"

It was an excellent point. Where was her laptop? She wasn't sure. Either back in her office or in the Sports and Social—assuming Archie hadn't already nabbed it.

She noticed that Angus from Accounts, conveniently seated alongside her, had no shortage of paperwork spread out in front of him, organised with an excessive supply of colourful sticky tags.

"I'm sure Angus won't mind if we share his papers, will you Angus?"

Angus smiled and nodded, moving them towards her.

Marlin was talking very carefully and self-consciously, trying to ensure her diction was free of any hint of slurring. There was less she could do however to mask the inevitable reek of Guinness that pervaded the room every time she spoke.

It was embarrassing, but far from unusual. After-lunch meetings were renowned for the varyingly intoxicated state of the attendees. Good sport was regularly had betting on who would turn up next and whether they'd be more pissed than everyone already present. It had become commonplace to keep a running score, assessing each successive arrival as they rolled into the meeting to help determine who would win the coveted 'Most Inebriated Attendee of the Day' award.

As if on cue, the door burst open and Sebastian van Goose staggered in, swayed for a moment in all his red faced, bleary-eyed glory, and then noisily and clumsily made his way towards the one remaining vacant chair. It couldn't have been in a less accessible and more awkward location if someone had planned it. Which possibly they had.

As Goose made his painfully erratic and unsteady passage around the room, he burped.

"Pardon."

And then he burped again.

"Bugger."

Squashing numerous attendees against the table as he pushed past—accumulating valuable extra inebriation points—Goose finally reached his destination, clattered down into the chair and started rummaging in his old fashioned leather briefcase for his laptop or papers or whatever else happened to be in it.

He hiccupped. And then he hiccupped again. And then he vomited abruptly and with admirable precision into the interior of his briefcase. Goose surveyed his colourful handiwork for a moment, as if contemplating a challenging contemporary work of art, and then snapped the briefcase shut, sat back and crossed his arms.

Marlin sighed with relief. She was officially no longer designated the most pissed person in the room. Goose had effortlessly taken the baton from her and was rapidly heading towards becoming the outstanding recipient of today's award.

Result.

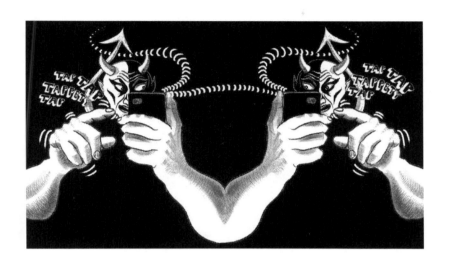

The Academics

P rofessor Noreen Doreen found her time increasingly occupied by her longitudinal study of the evanescent outpourings of social media. It was the self-obsessed Twitterati busy preening and indulging their fragile egos that most fascinated her. Her widely cited paper 'The Sociopathy of Social Media Mavens: Self-Gratification, Perceptions, Networks and Ecosystems' was widely regarded as the definitive study on the subject. It was an inspired title, one that worked so much better than her original choice—'Top Twats of Twitter.'

Her academic career was now lucratively dedicated to monitoring and analysing the Twitterati's fleeting and self-evident observations. As they were liked, retweeted and echoed in the timelines of their tribes, she observed how they clung to the delusion that they were shared moments of meaning, perception and significance. It provided a fascinating insight into the human psyche. More importantly, her ground-breaking research papers had enabled her to secure several significant and life-enhancing grants from her friends at Subsidies-R-Us, the government's 'innovation organisation' for funding academic old mates' obscure and pointless work.

She had watched with bemusement as many of the Twitterati had flocked to obtain the Officially Sanctioned 'Blue Tick', as if they needed it to reassure themselves they were indeed People Of Substance who created Tweets Worth Watching, missing entirely the irony that those with most to contribute had little need of such things. Twitter provided an alternative reality—or perhaps an alternative to reality—in which a few high-profile tweets were mistaken as more important than stepping away from their worn keyboards, pulling on their clothes and actually going outside and doing something useful.

The phenomenon of social media enthralled Doreen. So much so that she was writing a book about it. It would be a great book. A book that would lance the boil of social media and its shallowness once and for all. With luck, it would be serialised in bite-size chunks in a major Sunday paper. There was though, she had to admit (if only to herself), something morbidly fascinating about the pied pipers of Twitter, with their neuro-identical mobs of group-think followers attacking anyone or anything that threatened their narrow, mutual self-interests.

Her research and insights were proving invaluable to the House of Lords inquiry into Antisocial Media, which she was assisting as their Specialist Adviser. All of this bizarre daily gladiatorial spectacle of humanity eating itself online formed part of her study. But it was not a dry study-at-a-distance where she remained solely an observer. No, it was important to her analysis that she intervened and probed and stirred the Twitterati in order to test her ideas and hypotheses. She had created multiple fake accounts and personas, but her most commonly used were @InYerFace1023, @LiberteeGals99 and @Rscraper101.

She loved to throw the occasional Twitter bomb into others' timelines—an antagonising remark that, like a burning stick thrust into a hornet's nest, enraged and excited the fanatical bedroom keyboardists, who would tap deep into their brittle egos to swarm together in mutual hatred and loathing before unleashing a deluge of venom and spite and crude language at her in response.

There were one or two particular accounts of interest that she would focus on for her research and analysis—accounts that seemed to engage with her time and time again. Accounts that she would bait in return, albeit all within the strict ethical framework approved by Subsidies-R-Us.

Much of the evidence and analysis for her study was based on her own fake accounts and their interaction with three others in particular: @TruthSayer666, @chundamonsta69 and @Tintinsdad_3401. They provided exactly the evidence she needed to support the thesis underlying her book.

If she had been a more sensitive soul, the second-hand invective directed at her and her personas—everything from the predictable and wearisome 'c**t' to the tiresome 'fuckwit' (yawn), 'gash' (again?) and 'bitch' (feeble) to the more exotic 'beastie shagger', 'three nipple breaster' and 'Corbyn-sucker' (possibly the most insulting of them all)—might have distressed and upset her. Yet it was not the insults that interested her so much as exploring how inventive and depraved her detractors could be in the disciplined space of 280 characters.

In crafting their repugnant responses, the Twitterati swarms proved repeatedly and tirelessly that social media had little to do with the 'wisdom of crowds' or dialogue, diversity and democratisation. No, social media was as much about hierarchy, control and subjugation of non-conformists and heretics as all other means of communication that had gone before.

It was proof to Doreen of the Madness of the Mob, a reminder of why the real world had long since evolved structures and governance and protocols around constructive social behaviour. It was an insight into a time before humanity had evolved, of dog eat dog, when even a sitting US President could appear online to lie and fake things without any apparent accountability.

She turned to the draft pages of her book, staring brightly at her from her computer screen. "I, Twitterati." It was a name she liked. It had something of a classic aura about it. And books of course remained the most important means of knowledge and dissemination, even in the midst of the so-called 'digital revolution'.

This was going to be the definitive study of the phenomenon of the Twitterati. It would make her name. Who knew—maybe she, or one of her fake personas—would even acquire an Officially Sanctioned Blue Tick as a result? She smiled at the thought.

And started typing.

Professor Ned Nobbler found his time increasingly occupied by his longitudinal study of the evanescent outpourings of social media. It was the self-obsessed Twitterati busy preening and indulging their fragile egos that most fascinated him. His widely cited paper 'Social Media Influencers and the Sociopathy of Self-Promotion: A Framework for Perception and Impersistence' was widely regarded as the definitive study on the subject. It was an inspired title, one that worked so much better than his original choice—'Top Twitter Tossers.'

His academic career was now lucratively dedicated to monitoring and analysing the Twitterati's fleeting and self-evident observations. As they were liked, retweeted and echoed in the timelines of their tribes, he observed how they clung to the delusion that these were shared moments of meaning, perception and significance. It provided a fascinating insight into the human psyche. More importantly, his ground-breaking research had enabled him to secure several significant and life-enhancing grants from his friends at Subsidies-R-Us, the government's 'innovation organisation' for funding academic old mates' obscure and pointless work.

He had watched with bemusement as many of the Twitterati had flocked to obtain the Officially Sanctioned 'Blue Tick', as if they needed it to reassure themselves they were indeed People Of Substance who created Tweets Worth Watching, missing entirely the irony that those with most to contribute had little need of such things. Twitter provided an alternative reality—or perhaps an alternative to reality—in which a few high-profile tweets were mistaken as more important than stepping away from their worn keyboards, pulling on their clothes and actually going outside and doing something useful.

The phenomenon of social media enthralled Nobbler. So much so that he was writing a book about it. It would be a great book. A book that would lance the boil of social media and its shallowness once and for all. With luck, it would be serialised in bite-size chunks in a major Sunday paper. There was though, he had to admit (if only to himself), something morbidly fascinating about the pied pipers of Twitter, with their neuro-identical mobs of group-think followers attacking anyone or anything that threatened their narrow, mutual self-interests.

His research and insights were proving invaluable to the House of Commons inquiry into Antisocial Media, which he was assisting as their Specialist Adviser. All of this bizarre daily gladiatorial spectacle of humanity eating itself online formed part of his study. But it was not a dry study-at-a-distance where he remained solely an observer. No, it was important to his analysis that he intervened and probed and stirred the Twitterati in order to test his ideas and hypotheses. He had created multiple fake accounts and personas, but his most commonly used were @TruthSayer666, @chundamonsta69 and @Tintinsdad_3401.

He loved to throw the occasional Twitter bomb into others' timelines— an antagonising remark that, like a burning stick thrust into a hornet's nest, enraged and excited the fanatical bedroom keyboardists, who would tap deep into their brittle egos to swarm together in mutual hatred and loathing before unleashing a deluge of venom and spite and crude language at him in response.

There were one or two particular accounts of interest that he would focus on for his research and analysis—accounts that seemed to engage with him time and time again. Accounts that he would bait in return, albeit all within the strict ethical framework approved by Subsidies-R-Us.

Much of his evidence and analysis for his study was based on his own fake accounts and their interaction with three others in particular: @InYerFace1023, @LiberteeGals99 and @Rscraper101. They provided exactly the evidence he needed to support the thesis underlying his book.

If he had been a more sensitive soul, the second-hand invective directed at him and his personas—everything from the predictable and wearisome 'prick' to the tiresome 'prat' (yawn), 'fuckface' (oh dear, really?) and 'sheep shagger' (feeble) to the more confusing 'burst condom', 'goat-splitter' and 'Thatcher-fucker' (possibly the most insulting of them all)—might have distressed and upset him. Yet it was not the insults that interested him so much as exploring how inventive and depraved his detractors could be in the disciplined space of 280 characters.

In crafting their repugnant responses, the Twitterati swarms proved repeatedly and tirelessly that social media had nothing to do with the 'wisdom of crowds' or dialogue, diversity and democratisation. No, social media was as much about hierarchy, control and subjugation of non-conformists and heretics as all other means of communication that had gone before.

It was proof to Nobbler of the Madness of the Mob, a reminder of why the real world had long since evolved structures and governance and protocols around constructive social behaviour. It was an insight into a time before humanity had evolved, of dog eat dog, when even a sitting US President could appear online to lie and fake things without any apparent accountability.

He turned to the draft pages of his book, staring brightly at him from his computer screen. "You. Me. Twitterati" It was a name he liked. It had something of a classic aura about it. And books of course remained the most important means of knowledge and dissemination, even in the midst of the so-called 'digital revolution'.

This was going to be the definitive study of the phenomenon of the Twitterati. It would make his name. Who knew—maybe he, or one of his fake personas—would even acquire an Officially Sanctioned Blue Tick as a result? He smiled at the thought.

And started typing.

The Chief Executive

L ogan Dibber, Chief Executive of the Commission for Rustic Angling Practices, had learned the value of patience early in his career. Over many years he had whittled and honed it into an exquisite art.

Minor skirmishes and the odd battle lost were of little consequence in the context of his long path to victory. He found great satisfaction in watching those who believed they'd got the better of him prematurely celebrate their short-lived 'triumphs' with colourful bunting and cake. Only later would they discover to their dismay that Dibber would have the last and longest laugh.

Dibber had tirelessly fashioned and refined his leadership skills by studying and adopting the doctrines of the great Sun Tzu. It had enabled him to become a black belt in the direction of his opponents' fate. Today's latest examples of his prowess were spread out before him in the front-page headlines:

```
Logan Dibber praised for inspired leadership by MPs

CEO forces U-turn on failing government programme

Chief Executive to thank for miracle of the fishes

'Dibber is clearly in our favoured mystic quadrant,
contact  our  intern  for  further  information'  —
Senior Partner at McBarnacle and Snatch
```

He smiled and retrieved a bundle of papers from his office safe, flicking through them until he found his most recent Two Year Plan. It provided a finely detailed blueprint for the actions and decisions he'd tirelessly executed during the intervening eighteen months. It even included mock newspaper headlines, presaging almost word for word those in today's papers:

```
Chief Executive sails to the rescue — fishermen hail
their heroic saviour

Turn-around CEO is talk of the town

Force of nature Logan Dibber defeats dysfunctional
Whitehall
```

Everything had happened precisely as he'd calculated. All the blame for the failures and cost overruns of the programme had fallen on the digital tribe, and all the praise and recognition on him. All was good with the world.

His Two Year Plan was within a few months of its conclusion, but now was not the time to relax. He needed to guarantee that nothing would upset or overturn his imminent victory. Today's lunch with a journalist was one of several remaining steps to embed his success and ensure his plan reached its final jubilant coda.

The journalist was already seated at the table in Schäferhunds when Dibber arrived, two empty beer bottles in front of him. Either the hack had arrived prematurely early, or he was indulging a particularly acute thirst. Dibber suspected the latter.

He'd selected Bart Malmot from a long list of competing journalists clamouring to interview him—top household names from print, online, TV and radio; and trade writers from a mix of fishing titles along with those from the computer press and even 'Wonderful Whitehall—the Award Winning Official Journal of the Officials'. He'd chosen the lesser known and somewhat unpredictable Malmot for a very specific reason: Dibber knew that he could direct and manipulate him in a way that wouldn't be effective with other, more experienced hands.

The restaurant was Dibber's suggestion. Schäferhunds was an elegant art deco establishment set in the heart of Westminster. It was where politicians, celebrities, think tank employees and journalists relaxed together, enjoying the reliable dining experience and extensive wine list. More importantly, Dibber knew that his lunch would be witnessed by a variety of well-known and well-connected people. The resulting gossip and tittle-tattle would nurture and cultivate the glowing coverage already blanketing him, helping ensure the story of his success was not prematurely forgotten.

"Logan Dibber," he said briefly, shaking the awkward Malmot by the hand and taking the seat opposite him.

"Malmot, Bart Malmot," the journalist responded, snatching a quick nervous swig from his third beer and wiping the froth from his mouth with the back of his hand.

Dibber was impeccably dressed as usual. A well-cut suit, smart shirt and tie, highly polished black leather shoes, blow-dried hair, expensive if unsubtle masculine scent. There was nothing permitted to be out of place, neither in the way he appeared nor in the way he spoke. Everything was calculated and designed down to the smallest detail. Sun Tzu would have been proud.

The contrast with Malmot couldn't have been greater. He was as dishevelled and unkempt as usual, the distinct whiff of hemp-like substances emanating from his general direction.

Dibber was not impressed but neither was he surprised. A poor dress code was indicative of a sloppy, infantile mind. But today that did not matter. In fact, it was those precise qualities that led Dibber to select Malmot to conduct the interview.

The waiter brought their menus and the wine list.

"Would you care for an aperitif gentlemen?"

"Another beer," came Malmot's Pavlovian response, waving his near empty bottle for unnecessary emphasis.

"One of your excellent margaritas please, Johan," requested Dibber.

"Oh—what he said. One of those too," Malmot added. "And the beer of course."

"Of course." There was a brief flicker of what looked like emotion on the waiter's face before he turned and departed towards the bar.

"So, tell me. What would you like to know?" Dibber asked, pouring himself a glass of water.

"Everything," replied Malmot. "One moment."

He rummaged in a worn carrier bag with a faded Aldi logo before retrieving a battered notebook and see-through plastic ballpoint pen. Turning noisily through the pages, he eventually located one relatively free of his tiny handwriting.

"I'd like to get your take on what happened. Why the programme went wrong, what you did to save it. A bit of personal colour, if you like. I've read all the reports and Parliamentary committee inquiry transcripts, so I have a pretty good grasp of the whole thing, but it'd be good to breathe a bit of life into it, dig a bit deeper below the surface, get into the fear and loathing."

"I see," said Dibber. "Let me start by explaining why I've been so perfectly suited to the role, and how I managed to turn disaster into personal triumph."

"Yes, yes, that sounds perfect," Malmot responded, making a few illegible scribbles in his notebook: *Egotistical wanker.*

"It's simple. I deliver. I make things happen. That's what I do," observed Dibber. "I was never in favour of moving our services towards being 'digital', whatever that means. The work I oversee is super complex, not easily filleted into a few pretty computer screens."

"Oh. That's interesting. You don't buy all this 'digital revolution' stuff then?"

"Well, it may have its place, although I'm not entirely sure where that would be. I deal in data, facts and figures, not horsefeathers. I was never in favour of it. The resource I needed most, which I stated clearly at the beginning of the programme, was headcount, not a bunch of juvenile developers telling me that computer automation would magically improve things for our fishing communities."

The waiter returned to the table with their margaritas and a side order of beer.

"Your drinks gentlemen. Would you like to order?"

"We certainly would," replied Dibber before Malmot had a chance to think. "I'm on a tight schedule Johan. I'll just have a main and could you bring it expeditiously?"

"I shall speak with chef and see what's possible, Mr Dibber," Johan responded.

"Thank you. The fifty-day rump steak, medium, with thick cut triple-fried chips and spring greens please, Johan," requested Dibber. "And sauce Béarnaise."

"Of course. And for you, sir?"

Malmot was looking longingly at the menu, finding it hard to hide his disappointment. He'd been anticipating a full three courses and copious side dishes, along with lashings of drink. Now his basic Maslow's needs were in imminent danger of not being met.

"I'll have the same. But with ketchup instead of the Béarnaise, and skinny fries and no greens but extra fries instead, and maybe a bit of gravy," he said. "And can you bring a starter at the same time for me to have alongside?"

"Alongside?" Johan enquired.

"That's it. I was thinking of the crab and toast."

"The crab and toast. To come with the main."

"Exactly that," confirmed Malmot, pleased he'd rescued the food situation to his advantage. "Surf and turf. And can you make sure the toast is well done. White sliced bread, nothing fancy, a little bit carbon-y, but not burnt."

"Carbon-y but not burnt. White. Sliced. Bread." Johan repeated inscrutably and gathered up the menus. "And any wine with the meal, gentlemen?"

"A red, medium bodied. Whatever you recommend, Johan," Dibber responded.

"Thank you, sir. Glass or bottle?"

"Glass," said Dibber. "Bottle," said Malmot.

There was a momentary pause.

"A large glass of Pinot Noir each it is," Johan decided diplomatically, picking up the wine menu and moving promptly away.

"Where were we?" Malmot asked, squinting at his notes. All he seemed to have scribbled so far was a string of expletives and an aide memoire to collect his laundry from the service wash on his way home.

"We were exploring the vagaries of the so-called 'digital revolution'," Dibber responded, sipping his margarita.

"Ah, yes. Thanks. Surely you can't be denying the value of digital? Every organisation on the planet is busy using technology to modernise," Malmot observed. "You can't stay stuck in the past."

"Be careful what you wish for. 'Go digital' they told me. It will be cheaper, faster, better they said. Nonsense. It's cost us more—much more. We went well over budget. None of the business benefits were being achieved. You'll need to talk to the digital team to find out why that is. They're the ones who spent the money.

"That's not to say it's a complete disaster on the digital front. Of course not—once I intervened things improved. In the midst of chaos there is always opportunity. We now have a highly respected and award-winning portal. Users can log in to request a copy of the current status of their account. We print and post it out to them the following day. First Class. All very efficient. It's become an exemplar of transformation in Whitehall. Our best services by far are the ones focused on customers who prefer to use assisted digital or good old reliable paper."

"Assisted digital? What's that?" asked Malmot.

"Our premium rate telephone service."

"Telephones? Oh, a call centre."

"If you like. A call centre. If it ain't broke, don't fix it as Sun Tzu says. That's very much my philosophy too. Digital complicates things. It's an endless money pit, always wanting more funding to keep things updated, running to stand still. What we need are systems and processes built to last, not constantly tinkered with."

"If you don't believe in digital, what do you believe in?" Malmot inquired. With his margarita in one hand and beer in the other, he was finding it challenging to update his notes. Not that it mattered, he would colour in the necessary detail later.

"The old traditional methods are still the best and most reliable."

"Such as?"

Dibber smiled. "Our responsive design call centre is the most popular service. It sends out paper forms to be completed using good old-fashioned pen and ink. Far more effective than the website foisted on us by the digital team. That's not to say their work isn't pretty. But it's also pretty useless. No-one wants it.

"The real secret of our success is the complex case team. They do all the hard work. It's not something a computer system can do—it's not the way the process has been designed. The super complex cases are dealt with by our super complex super team. They know what they're doing. I can't replace them with a digital equivalent even if I wanted to. Complex and computers do not go together, trust me."

"I'm hearing that song by Frankie Goes to Hollywood in my head—'Two tribes'," commented Malmot.

"Two tribes? I don't know it. Music, the arts—not my thing."

"Two tribes go to war. Old school versus digital. Pistols at dawn. My way or the highway."

"If by 'old school' you mean I get things done while others simply chatter about things, or think about things, or put stickies on walls, or bunting around the office, then yes, I plead guilty as charged. My results speak for themselves. It's always better to lead than to follow. Everything I'm in charge of is rated green. But the digital aspects are red. Need I say more?"

"But it's government policy, isn't it? Digital by default. That's what Bacchus Jardine has said. Are you saying you don't follow government policy?"

"I'm doing what I was asked to do—deliver. Something that works. 'Customer first', that's the important thing. Digital is rarely the best way to do these things. It's a tool. But sometimes it's a tool best left in the bottom of the box, unused and unloved. That's why I took control. I was the only one capable of bringing it back on track. Since that moment, everything's run on schedule and to budget. More or less."

The waiter arrived accompanied by a server precariously balancing an outsized tray on his shoulder.

"Your lunch and your wine, gentlemen."

"Excellent. Thank you, Johan."

Their steaks were well-aged and succulent and deserving of their undiluted attention. They sat eating in silence for a time. Malmot was conflicted about how best to tackle the feast in front of him. He decided to alternate between the crab and toast starter and the steak, dunking both into the blended vat of tomato ketchup and gravy he'd created on his plate. Dibber was grateful they wouldn't be dining together again.

"If you find digital teams and systems and processes so unhelpful, exactly how did you deliver the programme?" Malmot asked, downing the remainder of his beer and margarita and glugging generously at his wine.

"Simple. Let me summarise my highly efficient and optimised approach for you. When the paper forms arrive in the post, our expert team opens the envelopes and enters the information into our well-established system. A second team checks that they have accurately copied the information from the paper forms into the system. Then a supervisory team checks that both teams are working to the correct standard, and we have a risk and audit team that conducts random sampling of the data and cross-checks it with the content of the original paper forms. It's all very finely tuned. All the necessary information is now in the system and we know it's accurate thanks to the elaborate processes I've established. Any errors that remain we attribute to the users who sent us the information in the first place. Users are always the weakest link, the fly in the ointment. Without them everything would run so much better.

"Look at it this way. When you drive a car, you don't do it with your head under the bonnet tinkering with the engine. So why should I do that with our programme? This digital nonsense puts all the focus on the engine and not on driving the car. I only wish I'd climbed into the driving seat and taken control sooner. It's always best to have a professional driver with a strong sense of direction who knows exactly where the car is heading. You can't indulge in constant debates with passengers otherwise you end up meandering and driving around in circles, lost forever in the middle of nowhere. That's digital for you."

"Why do you think you've been successful where others failed?"

"KISS."

Malmot blushed and averted his eyes from Dibber's penetrating stare.

"No, not kiss. KISS. In capitals," smiled Dibber. "Keep It Simple Stupid. That's the key. This online, interactive stuff is confusing and complicated. But a paper form has timeless elegance and simplicity. It endures. You can flick quickly between pages and find the information you need. Years later, decades later, you can pick it up and have instant random access. Show me any computer system that can do that. I've never experienced it. A so-called digital front-end is unnecessary fluff, a designer's ego-trip. Built in complexity, built in obsolescence. No-one needs it. No-one wants it."

"But what about these allegations of combative relations between you and the digital team? Of inappropriate personal behaviour and a frustrating, demoralising work environment?"

"The outcome speaks for itself. The rest is just chaff."

"But it's a very negative thing to have people saying about you," Malmot persisted. "People tell me you should have been fired, that even now you should be fired."

Dibber set down his cutlery and aligned it neatly on his empty plate. He reflected for a moment, taking a first sip of the Pinot Noir.

"That's the by-product of a fundamental misunderstanding. I won't sit here and criticise my digital colleagues for the way they indulge themselves in the exercise of power without responsibility. My advice to them would be to focus a bit less on being bleeding edge and a bit more on being leading edge. And leading is what I do. Paper-assisted digital—paper-powered digital—is where the game is now. Even the digital acolytes seem to accept that."

Malmot was surprised. "I don't understand. In what way?"

"Watch them in action, the way they work. Everything they do relies exclusively on pens and papers, and coloured sticky notes on walls. Filling in their little notebooks. Drawings on flip charts and white boards. The 'digital' presentations they do—short words in large fonts on plain backgrounds—are a rehash of old overhead projectors and foils. Nothing new. At the heart of digital is a reliance, a dependency even, on stationery. The hypocrisy of it all."

Dibber turned around at a perfectly timed moment as the waiter was passing. "Johan, the bill please."

"Sir."

"Oh," said Malmot half-heartedly, chewing on a generous mouthful of crab and steak and carbon-y toast and chips and ketchup and gravy. "I'll get lunch if you like. I can claim it on expenses from the editor."

"Not at all," Dibber replied. "I can't risk anyone suggesting I'm influenced by journalists buying me lunch, can I now? I'm a public servant. It's on me."

Malmot was mortified. If only Dibber had made clear at the start of the lunch that he was going to pay, everything would have been so different. Malmot had missed a vital and rare opportunity for bountiful free food and drink.

Johan placed the bill on the table. "When you're ready, Mr Dibber."

"It's been a pleasure discussing this with you, Mr Malmot," Dibber said, pushing back his chair and placing his perfectly folded spotless napkin on the table. "I'm sorry to be rude and leave when you haven't quite finished, but I'm sure you understand. I have important meetings this afternoon."

"Oh, it's no problem, no problem at all," Malmot assured him, his eyes fixed on Dibber's barely touched glass of Pinot Noir. "It's been very informative. Thank you."

Dibber nodded, picked up the bill and moved towards the bar area. Malmot sat finishing his plate of fusion cuisine. He watched as Dibber chatted briefly with the staff, paid and headed out of Schäferhunds. The moment he was gone, Malmot reached over and swapped his empty wine glass with Dibber's, taking a big gulp as he did so. Bliss. He detested people who ordered drinks and left them unfinished. It said everything he needed to know about their character.

The Maslow-challenging shortfall of lunchtime food and drink aside, Malmot was pleased with the interview. He'd played Dibber like a fool and obtained everything he wanted. 'Off the record' meant nothing to Malmot. They were empty words uttered at everyone he interviewed. Malmot was going to deliver the entire lunchtime conversation gift-wrapped to his editor, albeit 'spiced up' a little bit here and a little bit there. The story was going to be explosive. It would drive a deep chasm between the digital teams in Whitehall and the crusty old guard. Impact, that's what journalism is all about. An article without impact wasn't worth writing so far as Malmot was concerned. He finished the wine and scampered off in search of a drink and somewhere quiet to write his scoop.

Malmot would have been disappointed, and possibly shocked, to learn that his lunchtime interview and its headline-generating consequences had already been anticipated in great detail in Dibber's Two Year Plan. Dibber was well aware that Malmot's 'off the record' assurances were entirely hollow, solely intended to relax his victims into talking too much—into disclosing facts and details and personal asides that he would weave and embellish into a sensationalised story that leaned more towards fiction and fantasy than fact. It was not Dibber who had been played—but Malmot: all warfare is based on deception, and Dibber was its peerless master.

Malmot's contentious and fanciful article was exactly what Dibber desired. It would keep him and his work in the spotlight. Dibber was already widely recognised in Whitehall as the undisputed king of CRAP. Malmot's article would now help him prove it to the world.

The Old Hack

C hris 'Herring' Herrington watched Emmanuel Fedderby MP stumble drunkenly out of Stranger's bar and onto the terrace outside, his movements awkward and erratic like a puppet with broken strings and a cruelly sadistic marionettist. The MP had already been well established in Stranger's when Herrington arrived late in the afternoon, and it was now approaching eight o'clock. Even an old timer like Fedderby needed to call it a day occasionally.

Herrington lifted his pint of Federation Fragrant Frog in silent tribute to the MP's departure and turned to participate in the final out-of-tune chorus:

> *"Then raise the scarlet standard high,*
> *Within its shade we'll live and die,*
> *Though cowards flinch and traitors sneer,*
> *We'll keep the red wine flowing here."*

The cramped and crowded bar—rammed with politicians and their staff, journalists, Officers of the House and a few startled looking guests—erupted into more of a roar than a cheer at the song's conclusion, glasses and their contents lifted aloft or flying through the air, sodden beer towels waved as flags, streaming unidentified liquids across everyone and everything.

The unlikely coalition of politicians who'd sneaked their way behind the bar to serve drinks and lead the raucous singing now shouted *"Free beer!"*, leaving Refreshment Department employees desperately trying to contradict them and restore a sense of order.

Since the demise of the old press bar, Stranger's had become the go-to place for many journalists to hang out instead, jostling with the nearby Lion Rampant on Whitehall and the Marquis de Sade off Smith Square for their lucrative patronage. Although Stranger's was not exactly the most inviting or luxurious of places, it provided the convivial atmosphere unique to the best pubs, where people from a diverse variety of backgrounds would talk, debate, hug, cry, kiss, hug again, laugh and argue. Herrington couldn't think of any other environment where members of all political parties mixed together so freely, including prominent frontbenchers busy pouring pints behind the bar, cracking jokes and joining in a variety of political songs and sea shanties.

He checked his watch. It was time to move on. His old Fleet Street compatriots from the days of its glorious high-circulation zenith routinely drifted towards the Marquis later in the evenings to swap the newest political gossip and remember times past. It was often a sharp-witted if boozy gathering, a posse of political journalists and editors full of unlikely tall tales rooted in even more unlikely events that had actually taken place.

The pavements outside the Marquis were packed with drinkers, all talking loudly in a way that suggested many long hours had already passed since their first round. He pushed his way through the crowd to the interior, attracted the landlady's attention and was served long before many of those already swaying impatiently at the bar. Protecting his two pints of Voluptuous Vampire, he snaked back through the noisy throng to the standing area at the far end, joining several colleagues deep in conversation.

"Rubbish! Uriah Dregswill was a scoundrel and a cheat," one of them was insisting, leaning closely towards his drinking companions. "He claimed to be a well-meaning media proprietor. But look at what he did. Same as all the other rich bastards. Stole from everyone to line his own pocket. Unbelievable."

"Nonsense!" Herrington interjected, swallowing most of his first pint in one appreciative gulp. "In comparison to other press barons, Dregswill was a saint."

"Hardly a bloody challenge, Herring," came the cynical riposte.

"Yes yes, he had his faults too, but he did a lot of good. He gave the political left a voice in the mainstream media. An important, much-needed voice, fighting back against the distorting prism of the right wing press and their media barons."

"Oh bollocks! Smell the coffee Herring! He was a total bloody shyster. When the fat old lardster fell overboard from that glitzy yacht of his, he contributed more to rising sea levels than climate change ever has!"

"Well, say what you like. He put his money where his mouth was, fought for the needs of the working man, the working class. A true comrade, despite his occasional flaws. He certainly wasn't one of your usual billionaire media moguls. He provided a brave lone voice raised up against establishment bullies and cheats."

"Crook of the century more like. Fraud, theft. He looted his own newspaper's pension fund—hardly helping the workers was he? You know it was bad when even the Serious Farce Office woke up and started to stick their noses in."

This criticism of his hero and former Fleet Street employer was too much for Herrington. He pushed through to a nearby table, swept the empty glasses away and clambered aboard complete with the remains of his second pint.

"Arise ye workers from your slumbers, arise ye prisoners of want," he started to sing, raising his Voluptuous Vampire in the air and waving it in time to his tuneless rendition.

A big groan went up from his fellow political journalists.

"He's off on one."

"Aw, blimey. Not again!"

Mercifully, Herrington's singing was barely audible above the noise and commotion of the heaving, overheated pub. His tabletop cabaret appearances had become such a familiar occurrence that barely anyone took any notice.

"So comrades, come rally, and the last fight let us face."

As Herrington reached the chorus, he became increasingly red faced and more hesitant in his recital. His colleagues knew the signs well and moved forward to help him down before he fell.

"He was a good man, a good man, you know," Herrington kept insisting.

"Of course he was, Herring," a colleague responded. "As utter bastards go. Time to fetch you a cab I think."

"Now that is a very good idea, that is. I have an article to write—a treasure trove of top secret government information from a trusted source, you know," he slurred, tapping the side of his nose conspiratorially.

"Yes, yes, of course you do."

Herrington drained his glass as a couple of colleagues helped him outside through the crowds and hailed a passing taxi.

"What's wrong with him?" the cabby inquired, leaning out of his window to look the dishevelled Herrington up and down with suspicion laced with a hint of ritual contempt.

"Oh, he's just overcome with emotion at the memory of his old boss. Uriah Dregswill."

"Fatty 'Fat Bastard' Dregswill? I had him in the back of my cab once. Fat twat."

Even with the back door of the cab open, it was proving surprisingly difficult to manoeuvre Herrington inside and onto the back seat.

"Where do you live Chris?"

"Huh?"

"Your address. The driver needs your address. To get you home. You do have a home, I take it?"

"Fleet Street, that's the place for me!"

"No, not where your heart lives. Where *you* live Chris."

Herrington mumbled an address not far south of the river and collapsed onto the back seat where he started singing again: "Though cowards flinch and traitors sneer, we'll keep the red wine flowing here."

One of his minders closed the cab door, turned to the driver and handed him several worn tenners.

"Make sure he gets there in one piece, will you? Not that you can tell at the moment, but he's one of our top political journalists he is."

"Yeah? Well, he certainly ain't no fucking Sinatra, that's for sure."

The cabby set the meter running and drove off, taking the faint sound of Herrington's increasingly incoherent singing with him.

The Ex-Minister

April Hopehouse MP glanced out of her office window in Portcullis House, unable to resist the allure of the vista across the Thames towards the London Eye. She watched as tourists strolled along Victoria Embankment. Businesspeople scurried between meetings. Industrial and tourist boats motored along the river. The odd—and *very* odd—shouty, gesticulating demonstrator walked up and down like a stiff clockwork toy, parading their incoherent banners. Frustrated motorists fumed amongst slow-moving and overheated Boris buses. Cyclists weaved in and out of the gridlocked traffic—and occasionally resorted to the cycle lane in desperation.

Reluctantly she turned away and looked back down at her laptop screen. It was difficult to find the right words. Difficult to accept that her political life was approaching its end. Where had the years gone? Her Parliamentary career had started multiple elections ago, back in the days when her party stormed into office, youthful, optimistic and idealistic revolutionaries. What ridiculously naïve fools they had been, full of dreams and ambition and hope, and totally unaware of the pitfalls and heartache that lay before them.

Hopehouse had enjoyed operating the levers of power as a Minister, tapping into her first-hand experience of education and finally finding herself in a position to implement the essential changes and improvements that had long burned inside her. Yet the so-called Ministerial levers of power were often about as useful and effective as the rusty, broken and immovable levers of a long-abandoned railway signal box.

Despite the frustrations and disappointments of public office, Hopehouse had proved herself one of the more successful politicians of her generation—possibly not the highest of high bars to meet. The sweet and exhilarating taste of power now felt a lifetime ago, a faded memory from the days before their debilitating pre-election crisis and subsequent ballot box rout. It was sobering to be thrust back into opposition, to become once more a spectator rather than a sculptor of political events. No longer could she do justice to those she represented, or deliver on the aspirations that first inspired her into a life in politics.

The title 'shadow' spokesman was one of the most brutally accurate in Westminster. The role was a shadow indeed—bereft of weight, of authority, of power. Hopehouse now hovered unseen and ineffective in the wings, busy but inconsequential, like a shadow boxer throwing punches harmlessly in mid-air. She understood how a substitute must feel at a major sports game, left forever idling on the bench, condemned to watch and shout and gesticulate from the side-lines while all the action happens elsewhere.

The loss of Ministerial office was not her only frustration. The wearying drip-drip-drip of cynicism whipped up by the reactionary tabloids and anti-social media, the *'They're all the same'*, *'Snouts in the trough'* thoughtlessly parroted insults endlessly repeated by those with no idea what a life in politics involved, had worn her down. How much easier it must be to ceaselessly moan, knock, carp and criticise than try to improve the world. Almost everyone she encountered in politics had entered for the best of reasons, eager to make a positive difference—even if they often passionately disagreed about the best way of doing so.

She became aware of the loud *thump-thump-thump* of music from a nearby member's office and knew instantly who it was—a prominent government MP notorious for partying hard every night. Late each morning he would crawl—often quite literally on all fours—into his Parliamentary office still drunk or irrevocably hungover, and recuperate with the assistance of loud music and enough sausage rolls from Westminster station Greggs to feed a modest village. Later in the day there would be a generous hair of the dog in Stranger's bar, a *'wee dram'* or two or three to quench the thirst. The cycle would then be replayed day after day, week after week.

Writing her resignation was proving challenging—and not just because of the distracting noises-off, or the way her secure laptop kept hanging and crashing. *Kerching!* Being in government had been an exhilarating, uplifting time. A time when she could implement dramatic changes to lift up and improve people's lives. It was hard to explain the sheer buzz and adrenaline rush of being at the centre of national and international events to anyone outside of government—and the ever-present, gut-clawing imposter syndrome sense of apprehension and fear of failure.

Hopehouse had entered politics with her eyes open, well grounded. She'd never expected it to be simple, and her expectations were easily exceeded. The pragmatic approach, 'One day at a time', had served her well in her career before politics and even more so since. Many of the civil servants she worked with had performed miracles, enduring long hours and putting in the selfless commitment and personal dedication to make the near impossible happen.

Other officials however she'd found difficult and prickly to work with. Notable amongst them were a group of Permanent Secretaries from the 'Department of No'. While the best of the Perm Secs were exceptional, the less capable occupied their time engineering problems and distractions rather than solutions. They would do just about nothing in their power to help her, as if schooled at Dickens' Circumlocution Office and still keen to enshrine *'the express image and presentment of how not to do it'*.

She found it bitterly ironic to now witness that small cadre of reactionary and obstructive Permanent Secretaries retire and receive automatic knighthoods—or even ermine-trimmed peerages—and then rush towards the limelight, voraciously criticising elected politicians, pompously pontificating on what needed to be done *here*, what must be done *there*. And yet when they'd occupied the great offices of Whitehall, when they possessed the very real authority and power and influence to deliver change, they'd instead devised ever more convoluted ways by which she and other Ministers could be thwarted, denying the government's democratic mandate.

Hopehouse had nearly been hounded from office by one particularly scheming and manipulative Permanent Secretary. He'd reported her to the Head of Impropriety with false claims of bullying and intimidation. It was only when she provided verbatim meeting transcripts and recordings, made surreptitiously on the sage advice of Jacky McDaniels, a trusted and principled civil servant, that the opposite was revealed to be true. Not only had he lied about her behaviour, but behind her back he'd countermanded her instructions and reversed her policy decisions. That particular individual was spoken to 'in a tone of severe admonishment', promoted several increments and dispatched to another department to continue his 'good work'. It was disappointing, but no surprise, when she saw his name duly added to the conveyor belt of honours.

There was something that both saddened and annoyed her about former public servants rushing to park their privilege in the undemocratic House of Lords. She found it the most eccentric of places, an atavistic institution seemingly torn from the pages of a compendium of nonsense verse for children. Before becoming an MP, she'd experienced the Queen's speech at the opening of Parliament from a seat high in the visitors' gallery. It was a bizarre spectacle now stuck forever in her mind, a surreal, comical dream caught between Alice in Wonderland and a Christmas panto.

"*My Government will …*" the Queen had proclaimed.

"*Oh no it won't!*"—it had taken all of Hopehouse's self-discipline to prevent herself shouting her instinctive response across the crowded chamber

She'd watched, slack jawed, as the Rouge Dragon Pursuivant, holder of the badge Red Dragon Cadwallader, Silver Stick and Silver Stick-in-Waiting alongside Gold Stick and Gold Stick-in-Waiting formally paraded as if in some weird and psychotic choreographed dream sequence.

Was this *commedia dell'arte*-like performance truly what the Mother of Parliaments was all about? No wonder so much of the UK was in a terrible mess. The near hallucinatory experience had made her a firm advocate of radical reform of the second chamber—an ambition only fuelled by later witnessing the mockery of the routine elevation of retired and talentless 'Department of No' awkward squad members and nefarious political party financiers to its already overcrowded benches.

She paused and looked outside again, watching a group of tourists feed a flock of one-legged and club-footed feral pigeons alongside the river and conscious of the continuing and relentless *thump-thump-thump* of excruciating sounds from the neighbouring office. No wonder the MP was driven to drink—she would be too if she exposed herself to the same appalling music day after day.

Doubts continued to nag her. Was she doing the right thing? Why *was* she resigning? Frustrating as it was, opposition did still have an important purpose. If she stood down at the forthcoming election, how would she feel knowing that other political views—corrosive, antithetical, regressive views—would prevail? And that was just within her own party. Wouldn't a life outside of politics prove even more frustrating than a few more years spent in opposition, where at least the occasional criticism might hit home, might make the government wobble or even rethink its ideas?

With her practical experience of Ministerial office, she knew how to make significant progress second time around. To deliver on her promises more quickly and effectively. She knew which civil servants to have removed and which to request onto her team. She would surround herself with those who cared and those who delivered, those who were bold and who solved problems rather than creating them, and those who knew how to work and oil the byzantine cogs and gears of Westminster and Whitehall to make the right things happen.

The officials who'd graduated with honours from the school of circumlocution would be efficiently and ruthlessly bypassed. They would be assigned to work instead with her more idiosyncratic and iconoclastic colleagues—the populist political misfits whose intemperate, outdated and irrational ideas would be better left unrealised for the benefit of the country. In that role, the brigade of 'Department of No' officials could fulfil their true vocation and ensure nothing of any consequence ever happened.

Hopehouse changed her mind. She deleted her draft resignation. No. She wasn't giving in. There was work to be done. Important work. The time for feeling sorry for herself and maudlin self-indulgence had passed. For the moment at least. Her decision made, she breathed a long, long sigh, as if exorcising and expelling doubts from deep within her soul.

At that very moment, the view from her window transformed. The sun appeared, repainting the sky and the Thames an upbeat bright blue. She took it as a rare welcome omen. It was time to refocus her efforts on improving the opposition's attacks on the government, researching and developing policies the country needed while they were in opposition. Their time would come again.

But first she had one more immediate and pressing job to do. She headed out of her office and towards the *thump-thump-thump* thudding along the corridor.

Hopehouse hesitated outside the MP's room, knowing he might not welcome her intervention, or even take hostile exception. Yet she had to try. She knocked firmly on the solid wooden door, hoping to be heard above the noise. For a moment she thought her efforts had gone unnoticed. But then the noise stopped.

The door opened and the MP stood there. Dishevelled, red-eyed, overweight, stubble-chinned—and swaying slightly as if blown by an unseen breeze.

Hopehouse put out her arm to steady him.

"I've come to help. Can we talk?"

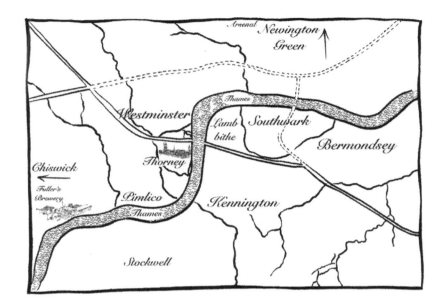

About the Riverbank

The riverbank referred to in this novel's title is that of the Thames as it passes through Westminster—home to some of the UK's most famous institutions, including the Houses of Parliament and Westminster Abbey. While today Westminster is a defining part of central London, it's situated upstream and to the West of the original mediaeval heart of the City of London.

Much of Westminster was once marshy, waterlogged land. At its centre was Thorney Island, formed by rivulets of the mighty river Tyburn as it met the Thames. According to King Offa, one-time King of Mercia, it was 'a terrible place'. Some would claim it still is.

It was Thorney Island on which Westminster Abbey and the Houses of Parliament were built. Later, as the Tyburn was tamed, culverted and built over, the island disappeared beneath the streets. Now only the name of nearby Thorney Street is a small reminder of what once was.

About the Author

Jerry Fishenden is a technologist, writer and composer. He's worked in and around Westminster, Parliament, Whitehall, the City of London and big and small businesses for longer than he cares to remember.

About the Illustrator

Clive Edwards worked for a broadcaster. He's interested in all sorts of stuff, but prefers not to go on about it. He likes drawing and is looking forward to a haircut.

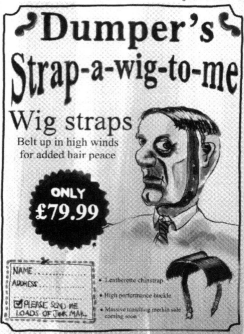